Georgiana M. Craik

Playroom Stories

Or, How to make peace

Georgiana M. Craik

Playroom Stories
Or, How to make peace

ISBN/EAN: 9783743407886

Manufactured in Europe, USA, Canada, Australia, Japa

Cover: Foto ©Andreas Hilbeck / pixelio.de

Manufactured and distributed by brebook publishing software (www.brebook.com)

Georgiana M. Craik

Playroom Stories

PLAYROOM STORIES;

OR,

HOW TO MAKE PEACE.

BY

GEORGIANA M. CRAIK,

AUTHOR OF 'LOST AND WON,' 'MY FIRST JOURNAL,' ETC.

ILLUSTRATED BY C. GREEN AND F. W. KEYL.

LONDON: GRIFFITH AND FARRAN,
(SUCCESSORS TO NEWBERY AND HARRIS)
CORNER OF ST. PAUL'S CHURCHYARD.
MDCCCLXIII.

EDINBURGH : PRINTED BY R. AND R. CLARK.

TO

HELEN AND HENRIETTA HUNTER,

IN MEMORY OF

HAPPY DAYS AT DEAR CRAIGCROOK.

CONTENTS.

—◆—

PLAYROOM STORIES.

WHY THE STORIES WERE TOLD.

IT was raining, and the children were at play all over the room; not a corner was free from them except the one corner where A. Z. sat at work. Tom was in a fortified castle besieged by Dick and Frank, and the battle-cries of these three almost drowned the smaller clamour that proceeded from Peggy as she whipped her doll, and from Kitty who ran races round the table, and from little Gracie who lay on the floor and screamed into the kitten's ears; but all together, they made such an uproar that at last A. Z., sitting at her work, said resolutely to herself, "This will *never* do!"

Now A. Z. was not the mother of these wild

young colts, and how much they screamed, or fought, or besieged one another's castles, was, in general, very little matter to her; but she had come for one week to take care of them while their mother was away, and for this one week, therefore, their way of going on concerned her very much indeed. She rather suspected, too, that they were going on in a way a good deal unlike their usual one (as small people sometimes will attempt to do when they get a new hand over them), and A. Z., though she was very good natured, did not feel a bit inclined to put up with this; so, when she had borne all the noise around her for about half an hour, she very decidedly made up her mind that she would bear it no more. The only difficulty was to know how to *help* bearing it; but A. Z. thought over the matter for a minute or two, and hit upon a plan for procuring peace which she thought would do; so—at the moment when the assault of the castle was at its very fiercest, when the long-enduring doll in Peggy's arms was suffering its very sharpest whipping, when Kitty, running races round the table, had run herself into that state when it is difficult to stand upright, and little Grace, upon the floor, had screamed so loud that the kitten had set up her back in kittenish fear of her life—at that very moment up sprang A. Z. from her chair, and stood upon it.

"Silence, boys and girls!" said A. Z.

There was no need to say another word; they were all as silent in a moment as if they had been shot. Dick and Frank let fall the battering-ram with which they had been going to bring instant ruin and destruction upon Tom; Tom saw himself rescued from annihilation, and failed to take advantage of his good luck; Peggy, forgetting every dictate of humanity, let her doll drop into the air suspended by one leg; as for Kitty, she fell plump upon the floor, and little Grace lost her presence of mind to such an extent that even the kitten perceived it, and, taking advantage of her, made her escape and fled. You see they were all quite used to one another's leaping on the chairs, but they were about as little prepared for a thunderbolt to fall upon them as for A. Z. to jump up on one.

So A. Z. cried "Silence!" and in one moment they all sat or stood as mute as mice.

"Now, I have something to say to you," spoke A. Z. "We must come to an understanding together, or we shan't keep friends. You three over there—Dick, and Tom, and Frank—do you think I am stone deaf?"

Well, no, they didn't think that certainly, but, as they each felt a little twitch of conscience at the question, they were none of them in a particular hurry to answer it. Dick, indeed, turned his back instead of saying anything, and Tom began to twirl his thumbs, and Frank, who was a shamefaced little fellow, blushed and hung his head. So, when nobody said a word, A. Z. went on.

"And you three girls," said A. Z., "what do you think I'm made of?"

There was even less chance of getting an answer to this question than to the first. All the girls stared in A. Z.'s face. Gracie's mind, for a moment, suggested "sugar-candy," but the idea was too wildly delicious to be retained.

"You know very well what I mean," continued A. Z. "You have been making an uproar as if all six of you were at the building of Babel. Now, once for all, boys and girls, it can't go on!"

Upon which there was a murmur from the besieged castle, and —

"*What* can't go on?" cried Tom, foremost in mutiny.

"Sieges, conducted with battering-rams, to begin with," answered A. Z. promptly. "The next battering-ram you make you may drive against some other wall than this, Master Tom. I'll have no more sieges here. So, I say again, it can't go on! If I could I'd send every one of you out of doors."

"Why, it's raining!" cried Dick, triumphantly.

"But it's raining!" echoed Frank and Peggy piteously; and Kitty, who had tumbled on the floor, began to cry.

"I *know* it's raining," answered A. Z. "Isn't that the very reason why I *don't* send you? But what I say is this—until it leaves off raining you shall carry on no more sieges."

"Then we had better give them up altogether," said Tom, sitting down inside his castle in gloomy despair, "for it rains always."

"Oh, it doesn't, Tom! it didn't rain yesterday," said truthful Frank.

"You hold your tongue!" cried Dick; and he made a sally upon Frank and routed him.

"Silence again! This won't do," said A. Z.

The silence was not quite so profound this time. Dick, indeed, having vanquished Frank, had no particular objection to a moment or two's truce; but Tom, sitting inside his castle, unsoothed by any conquest, called out bluntly—

"What do you want?"

"I'll tell you what I want," answered A. Z. "I want peace. You may make what noise you like out of doors, but now and henceforward I mean to have peace within. You have been taking advantage of me. You have been imposing on me; and now I'm going to impose something upon you. Dick," said A. Z., suddenly descending from her chair, and bringing all eyes upon herself again, " Dick, come here, and I 'll tell you a story."

" What for ?" demanded suspicious Dick.

Why do you pick out Dick ?" cried Tom.

" Oh, couldn't you tell a story to us all ?" cried Kitty, sitting on the floor.

" No," answered A. Z. ; " my story is for Dick. You may listen if you like—that 's no concern of mine—but I'm going to tell the story to Dick.   Sit there, Dick," said A. Z., pointing to a seat exactly opposite her own.

Now Dick, having that seat so pointed out to him, did not feel greatly moved to take possession of it, and if it had not been that he was not a very big boy, though he was the eldest of the six, I almost think he would have said, " I won't," when A. Z. called him to it ; but not being very big, and feeling, therefore, undecided in his mind, he began to temporize.

" I can hear you where I am," said Dick.

" Very likely ; but you're too near Tom," said A. Z.

" Then Tom can move," said Dick.

" And so can Dick," said A. Z.

And then Dick, feeling that the matter was going against him, began to do what he was bid.

" Now, let no one disturb us," said A. Z. " Dick, are you ready ?"

" Yes," answered Dick uneasily.

And then A. Z. began.

STORY THE FIRST.

THE GIANT.

PART THE FIRST.

ONCE upon a time [said A. Z.

"I hate stories that begin 'Once upon a time,'" said Tom, beginning, in sign of contempt, to pound the castle chairs.

"Who was speaking to you, Tom?" asked A. Z.]

Once upon a time there was a giant—·

["Oh! oh! it's going to be a fairy story!" cried little Grace, clapping her hands.

"Are *giants fairies*, stupid?" demanded injured Dick.

"No more interruptions, boys and girls," said A. Z.]

Once upon a time there was a giant who lived

in a cottage in a very great wood. Now giants were not very common in those days, and the giant's father, when he built the cottage, had quite forgotten to make it big enough for a giant to live in com fortably—which was a great mistake, you know. So when the giant was born they hardly knew what to do with him. The mother had got a cradle ready, but of course he wouldn't go into that. They had to put him in their own bed, and they themselves had nothing for it but to lie on the floor. "It's very awkward, indeed," said the giant's father, when he saw what had to be done ; and so it was, but you see there was no help for it. So they made up the best bed they could for themselves on the floor, and had to be content with it.

Well, the large bed did very well for the giant for a little while, but, before many days were over, he began to grow so fast that they saw *that* would not hold him very long. "We shall have to put *him* on the floor," said the father, then, with a chuckle : "it's the only place large enough for him." And to be sure, before a couple of months were over, they *had* to put him on the floor, and then they got back to their own bed again.

I don't think that there ever before was a giant that grew so fast ; you might have sat beside him and have seen him grow. "He's three quarters of an inch taller since morning," his mother would say constantly as she put him to bed, and you may fancy whether or not she was proud of him. She used to measure him every night and morning, and make a little mark on the floor at the point which his feet reached.

Though you would hardly believe it, however, the giant's father was by no means so pleased as his wife was with this big son.

" What on earth are we to do with him ?" he would often say as he sat and looked at him. " Was there ever such a monster born before to a poor man !" And, instead of being grateful, he would think of nothing but what it would cost to feed and clothe him. For, to tell the truth, it cost a good deal to do that even now, as the giant was seldom content unless he was putting something into his mouth, and I hardly like to say how many loaves his mother had to cut up every day to make bread and milk for him ; for as to letting him cry for anything without getting it, you would only need to have heard him cry once to feel that *that* was out of the question entirely ; and then as to clothes, why the buying of them seemed never to cease, for though, of course, his mother put deep tucks into all his petticoats, yet he grew out of them almost quicker than she could make them up. So it was a heavy expense, and the giant's father had to work harder at his wood-cutting (for that was his occupation) than he had ever worked before in his life.

Of course the giant's mother had her hands full too, for it was no joke to take charge of such a boy as hers. Though he was so big, he couldn't do a bit more for himself than other children, and it was a year and four months before he ever stood on his feet; and as for speaking, he was full two years old before he could say a single word plainly.

"Let him alone; he'll talk soon enough," his father always used to say with a groan; and to be sure they *did* find that it was soon enough when he began to speak at last, for the first time he said "Dadda!" six of his mother's best dishes fell flat down upon the floor at the noise.

When he began to walk, of course the house wouldn't hold him. He always had to creep on his hands and knees out at the door, and get himself quite free of it before he could stand up. I told you that the cottage stood in a wood, and when he was learning to walk his mother found the trees there very useful indeed, for instead of steadying himself by her like other children, which never would have done at all, you know (she did try to hold him up once, and, at the first stumble he made, down she went like a nine-pin), he used to grasp a tree round with each of his arms, and in that way tottered on from one to another, and taught himself to walk so well that by the time he was three years old there was scarcely anything that could have thrown him off his feet. "He's as steady as a house—the darling!" his mother used to say; and he really was.

I am sorry to be obliged to confess that as the giant grew up he did not become exactly what you would call a nice boy. The fact is, he was spoiled at home. For, if you come to think of it, you will find that it must be a very difficult thing to bring up a giant well. He is so big, you see, that you don't know what to do with him. As for beating him when he goes wrong, of course *that* is quite out of the question. You can't very well even talk to him, because the chances are he'll cry if you do, and I know I for one would not like to talk long with a giant blubbering at my side. Then, as for shutting him in a room alone to think seriously over his faults,—why, so far as *our* giant is concerned, there was only one room in the cottage, and not so much as a key to the door of that, so it was quite useless to think of locking him up. The result was, therefore, that the giant grew up having so much of his own way, that by the time he was six or seven years old he was a perfect Turk. There was no living with him except by humouring him.

He used to keep his mother on the tramp for him from sunrise to sunset; and as for his father, things came in a few years to such a pass that he hardly knew how to call his ears his own.

You may be sure, too, such being the state of things at home, that the giant thought no little of himself; indeed, he thought so much of himself that he never was known to think of anything else. He thought of himself when he rose in the morning, and he thought of himself when he went to bed at night, and all day long he used to think in his heart —" Surely such a fine giant as I never was born!" But I must say in excuse for him, that if he went on in this way it was not very much wonder, for his mother spent the whole of her time in shewing him what a fine fellow he was, and of course nobody can say that it was not natural in him to believe what his mother said.

Well, time went on, and years passed, and the giant grew bigger and bigger, and the bigger and the stronger he grew the lazier he grew too. He would not work so much as a stroke for his living— not he. Giants were not so common that they need be set to slave like other people, he would say; and day after day he would let his father go off with his axe upon his shoulder into the wood, and never so much as once say to him—" I'm stronger than you, father; I'll come and fell the trees." No; he used to stay at home, and lie out in the sunshine, and eat and drink and sleep all day, and never from year's end to year's end did a good turn to anybody.

All this time he had gone on sleeping on the cottage floor, because you see his father and mother had never been able to afford to buy a bed big enough for him, and his mother had added one mattress to another until at last they stretched the whole length of the cottage—and it was not a small one—from end to end. But at last, when the giant was about thirty feet high, even this would not do for him any longer. One night when the father and mother were in bed they were awakened by a great tramping against the walls,—and what do you think this was? It was nothing but the giant stretching out his legs.

"The poor dear boy! he'll knock his feet into blisters," said his mother, when she had looked out and seen what it was.

"The 'poor dear boy' will knock the house wall down," grumbled the father, turning over on his side, and going off to sleep again.

But the mother lay awake all the rest of the night thinking what could be done, and in the morning when she went to kiss her son, and ask him how he had slept (which she never did till the father had had his breakfast and gone off to work, because the giant didn't like to be disturbed early),

"My dear boy," said she then, "I'm afraid you had a very uncomfortable sleep last night."

Now the giant had not been conscious of being uncomfortable at all, but, as he never liked to lose an opportunity of being pitied, he first stared in her face, and then he said—

"I daresay I had,—only I was asleep, and I don't remember it."

"Ah, my dear, but *I* wasn't asleep," answered the mother, "and I saw how uncomfortable you were with your feet. Why, you can't put them out."

At which the giant in a fright, thinking that something ailed his limbs, instantly with all his might began to stretch them, and of course they struck immediately with a greater noise than before against the wall. The shock (for it quite shook the cottage) threw the mother down, but, as she only fell on the mattresses, she soon picked herself up again, before her son had finished grumbling.

"What on earth's to be done now?" said the giant.

"My dear, that's just what I've been thinking for hours," answered the mother.

"Father must build a new house," said the giant.

"That he never will do," answered the mother.

And upon that the giant began to howl.

"There never was anybody treated like me. Nobody thinks of anything but themselves. I might be dead for anything you would care. Aw! aw!" howled the giant.

And then of course the mother began to cry too, and, as she always did whenever he made her cry, she commenced giving in to him as fast as ever she could.

"I 'll ask father to build a new house," she said.

"Aw! aw! I don't care!" blubbered the giant.

"I 'll speak to him about it this very day," said the mother.

"You may do as you like," answered the giant.

"My boy shan't lie at night and blister his feet," said the mother.

"You don't care whether I blister both head and feet too," answered the giant.

However, at last she got him into rather a better humour, and it was settled between them that as soon as ever the father came from the wood they should ask him to build a new house.

So when the father returned to his dinner—

"Father," said his wife, as she handed him a bowl of soup, "we 've been thinking that you will have to take a few weeks soon, and build us a new house."

Now, though the mother said this so coolly, yet all the time she spoke she was trembling in her shoes, for she knew very well what sort of an answer she was likely to get. And I can tell you she was not mistaken, for the father set down his spoon, and up he lifted his head, and—

"What nonsense are you talking now?" said he. "Build a new house! Is the old one falling to pieces?" and he gave her such a look that it nearly knocked her down.

"Well, no—no, not exactly falling to pieces," she answered; and her voice went up and down so, because she was in such a tremble, that you could scarcely hear what she said; "not exactly falling to pieces, father, but it's so small, you know, that the poor dear Giant can't get his proper night's rest in it."

"Oh—the Giant can't get his proper night's rest in it, can't he?" said the father, and with that, up he got from his seat, though he hadn't eaten a mouthful of his dinner yet, and with his face so swelled with the rage he was in that it was near double its ordinary size. "He can't get his proper night's rest in it, can't he?" he said. "Then tell him he may try what kind of rest he can get *out* of it—the idle, lazy, good-for-nothing rascal!"

And with that he dashed out of the cottage, leaving the whole of his dinner behind him.

Then, as you may suppose, the mother began to cry, and she cried and groaned so loud that the giant, who was lying under half a dozen trees in the wood, presently heard the noise she made, and shouted out to know what the matter was; and when she went to him and told him (and she repeated every word that his father had said, and a few more), you can fancy what a temper he was in. He called his father all the wicked names that he could think of, and went on in such a way all through the afternoon that the mother at last was quite at her wit's end to know what to do with him.

While this was going on at home, the father, working in the wood, was thinking over what his wife had said, and wondering very sorrowfully what it would be best to do. For you see he had never, as the mother had, been able to fall down and adore the giant; for his own part, he didn't care for giants; from the very first, when he had had to give up his bed to him, he had felt that a giant in the house would be very much in the way. He had been very comfortable at home before the giant was born. In those days his wife used to have nothing else to think of but him, and he never came from his work but he would find her standing at the door in her neat clean gown, ready to smile at him and welcome him back, and she would sit beside him in the evenings with her work in her hands, prattling to him so kindly ; but all this had come to an end at the giant's birth ; he had come between them, and spoiled her love for him from the very hour he was born.

It had been a hard life for the poor father ever since. Up early and down late—working hard all day—and little to get for it but cold looks at home, for, you see, work as hard as ever he liked, he never brought home enough to satisfy the giant ; and as for his wife (though it was no fault of hers) the poor woman had never had a new best gown to her back since the giant had come into world.

So the father, as he worked this afternoon, thought of all these things, and of what a long weary struggle it had been, and the more he thought of it the sadder and sadder he got, for he felt like one who had had a burden strapped upon his back which was every day getting heavier and heavier, and which he saw no way of ridding himself of. And the more he thought the sadder he got, and he could hardly go on working at last, he was so sorrowful and weary at heart.

But when it had become evening, and he turned

on his way home, suddenly as he walked along this
sadness passed away from him, and quite an unex-
pected cheerfulness and hopefulness came over him.
It was as if he had come out from a dark lane into
bright sunshine.   He walked along, and thought,
and laughed to himself.   " Who knows ? " he said
once ; " the old days may come back yet."   Then
he began to think of them again, and went along
smiling.

When he reached the cottage, he found it all
quiet, and going in softly he found that his wife and
the giant had both fallen fast asleep (for they had
had such an afternoon of it together, you know, that
they were quite worn out).   So he went to the bed
where his wife lay, and threw a cloak over her to
keep her warm, and then, for he felt very kindly to
her, he stood by her side and looked at her face, which,
as she lay sleeping so calmly, seemed to have grown
younger, and as he looked he smiled again, for he
could almost think that she was his young kind
wife returned to him.   Then he went and softly
raked the coals together, and sat down by the fire-
side thinking.

When he had sat so for about half an hour the
giant gave a groan, and turned round and opened
his eyes.

Now, as you know, the giant had been in a great

rage with his father all the afternoon, and so I daresay you think that when he awoke and found him
so close to him, he would begin to say a few of those
things to his face that he had been saying so freely
behind his back ; but he didn't do so at all. The
fact is, though the giant was such a big strong fellow, he was *always* much fonder of saying things
behind people's backs than to their faces. He was
a prudent giant, and liked to take care of himself
and keep out of harm's way ; so when he awoke just
now and saw his father sitting by the fire, instead of
repeating a word of all those he had been saying so
glibly during the afternoon, he just squeezed his
knuckles into his eyes, and then looked out again,
and said sulkily—

"Oh, you 've come back—have you ? "

"Yes, Giant, I 've come back," answered the
father quite cheerfully.

And then the giant hadn't another word to say,
but sat up on one elbow and stared before him into
the fire.

So when this had gone on for some time, and the
father saw that the giant was well awake, he all at
once began again.

"Giant," he said ——

["Hadn't the giant got a name, A. Z. ? " asked
Frank.

"No," answered A. Z.; "he was just called 'Giant.'"]

"Giant," said the father, "it's queer how one takes to dreaming sometimes about old things. What do you think has been running in my head while you have been asleep?"

"How should I know?" answered the giant surlily.

"The days when I was a boy—that's what I've been thinking of," said the father. "One time in particular — dear, dear! what a merry time that was!" And then the father leant back in his chair, and off and on for the next minute or two there he lay chuckling.

Well, you can't think how that aggravated the giant. He glowered at his father under his heavy black eyebrows, and the more the father laughed and seemed to enjoy himself, the angrier he became, till presently he got quite red with rage.

"You needn't keep all the fun to yourself," he grumbled out at last, and with that the father turned to him again quite good humouredly, and——

"No, my boy, that's true," he said, "for it isn't much that falls to your luck here. Things were different with me, Giant, when I was a boy. I wouldn't have stood a life like this — bless you, no!"

"What sort of a life *had* you then," said the giant sulkily, "if it wasn't like this?"

"The right sort, my lad," answered the father. "Plenty to do and see—plenty to eat and drink—and no end of fun. What d' you think I did once for a bit of fun, Giant?"

"*I* don't know," said the giant surlily; but, though he pretended not to care about hearing, he pricked up his ears.

"Ran away!" said the father. "What d' you think of that?"

Well, the giant didn't quite know what to think of it, but as his father was waiting for an answer—

"Depends upon what you did next," he said prudently.

"That's true; so it does," answered the father. "Now what do you *think* I did?"

"Lost yourself?" suggested the giant, after a little reflection.

"Why, what would have been the fun of that?" said the father. "No. Fell in love!"

He gave a look towards the bed as he spoke, but the mother was quite fast asleep.

"Fell in love!" echoed the giant. "Who with?"

"Well, I'm not quite sure, Giant," said the

father, "but I think"—and then he dropped his voice—"I *think* she was a princess."

"A princess!" exclaimed the giant, and you may fancy how he opened all his eyes.

"Yes, I think she was a princess," said the father. "She had a gold crown on her head, and as for jewels, why, you'd have thought she was jewels all over. It was as much as you could do to look at her."

"Why?" said the giant.

"Because she glittered so," answered the father. "It was like coming beside one of the stars. You never saw anything like it, Giant!"

There was no denying that; the giant had certainly never seen anything like it at all. He began to scratch his head thoughtfully when his father paused.

When they had both been quiet for a few moments—

"And how did you lose sight of her?" said the giant.

"Ah!" answered the father, and he shut his eyes, and began to shake his head slowly up and down. "When I think of it, Giant!"

"What *is* it you're thinking of?" roared out the giant.

"How they found me, and took me home," said the father. *That's* what I'm thinking of."

And then he began to groan.

"Well, it's all very fine," said the giant, after he had thought again for a little, "to talk of what *used* to be. Things aren't now as they used to be. There's no princesses now—nor anything else."

"What! no princesses?" said the father, opening his eyes as if he had never been so surprised at any remark in his life. "Well!" and he nodded his head up and down, "*try* if there aren't."

"*I* don't know where to try," said the giant sulkily.

"Oh, *I'm* not going to tell you," said the father. "There were princesses, and heaps of things, in my time. Why, the world's *full* of wonders! But nobody asks *you* to go and look for them. Heaps of wonders!" repeated the father; but with that, all at once, he fell into such a dreadful fit of coughing, that the noise he made woke the mother; and then, as you may suppose, there was no more talk of princesses that night.

But, for the first time in all his life, when he went to bed that evening, the giant couldn't sleep. There he lay, rolling and tossing, and nothing could he think of but princesses with crowns on their heads, and all the other fine things that there must be in the world. " Princesses, and heaps of wonders!" that was what his father had said, and you can't think how the words rang in the lazy giant's ears. " What a wonderful place the world must be!" thought the giant to himself.

By the time the morning had come, I think you can guess what the giant had determined to do. He had made up his mind that he would set out that very day, and see what the world was like. You must know that he was so lazy that he had never yet gone out of the wood, and had no more idea of what was beyond it than you have, but he felt now that he could not possibly live another day without finding out. He was even in such a hurry to set off that he got up an hour earlier than he had ever done in his life before, quite giving his mother a turn, as you may fancy, when she saw what he was about.

However, he didn't say a word to her about what he was going to do until he was dressed and had had his breakfast, and then, all at once, as she was beginning to wash up the cups and saucers—

" Mother," said the giant, " how many loaves have you got in the house ?"

" Loaves ?" said the mother, and she stared at him quite astonished ; but she went to the pantry and counted them, and said, " fourteen." (For you know the giant had such an appetite that they were always obliged to keep a good supply.)

"I'll take them," said the giant then.

"You'll take them *where?*" cried the mother.

"Into the world; I'm going to see it," said the giant.

And then the mother set up such a scream that you might have heard it half through the wood.

However, the giant didn't much mind screaming, so, while she was recovering her breath, he went away to the pantry, and packed up the loaves. He tied them all up in a great towel, and slung them round his neck, and then he went up to his mother, and said coolly—

"Now, I'm off."

But the poor mother was sobbing as if her heart would break.

"Oh, Giant, Giant, stay one other day," she said.

"I won't stay another hour," said the giant.

"It'll kill me! I shall never get over it!" cried the mother.

"Oh, stuff and nonsense!" said the giant.

And then he kissed her, and said good bye to her, and before she could even ask him if he would ever come back again, he had shut the door and was gone.

The first thing he did was to go through the wood to where his father was at work. When he came to him—

"Hallo!" said the father, pretending to look surprised, "where are *you* off to, Giant?"

"I'm going into the world," said the giant.

"No!—you don't say so?" cried the father.

"Yes, I am," said the giant.

"Going to look for princesses?" said the father.

"I shouldn't be the first if I was," answered the surly giant.

"That's true, Giant," said the father. "Well, I hope you'll find one;" and then he gave a great chuckle.

"Good bye," said the giant.

"Good bye," answered the father; and they shook hands.

"Don't give up if you shouldn't find her just at first," called out the father.

"All right!" said the giant; and away he went.

"Now, Dick," said A. Z., breaking off, "we'll stop here."

"But it isn't the end!" said Dick sharply, in a tone of injury.

"It can't be *near* the end!" chimed in Kitty and Frank.

"No, it isn't the end, but the end will keep," said A. Z. "We've had enough of it for one day."

"It's a funny story, A. Z.," said little Gracie, not quite sure whether she liked it.

"*I* think it's nonsense!" said Tom boldly.

"Oh, Tom!" cried Frank, and Kitty sitting still upon the floor.

"*Did* he ever find the princess, A. Z.?" asked Peggy thoughtfully.

"I couldn't possibly tell you to-day, Peggy," answered A. Z.

"Did he ever come upon any *castles?*" demanded Tom, who was still perched inside his.

"I shouldn't wonder that he did," said A. Z.

"Why do you say you 'shouldn't wonder?' As if you didn't *know!*" cried Tom indignantly, conscious of equivocation.

"I *don't* know," answered A. Z.

At which they all stared at her, but A. Z. only laughed and rose up.

"Away! off with you, every one. The rain's at an end!" she cried.

The rain *was* at an end to be sure, and they all ran off into the open air, and left A. Z. a quiet hour before tea.

THE GIANT.

PART THE SECOND.

THERE was school in the mornings, for a longer or shorter time, for all the children except little Grace, so A. Z. got on very well next day till after dinner. The boys, who were kept longest at their lessons, came home to dinner at three, and then when that was over there was play for everybody. The room in which they usually sat in the afternoons when they were indoors was a large parlour very plainly furnished, so that the romps of the boys might not do much mischief; and here on the afternoon of this day they all gradually assembled, dropping in one by one, when dinner was ended. It was rather a cold gloomy sort of day, and the ground was very wet, for it had been raining all night.

A. Z. sat down and took out her work. The boys were standing about looking out at the windows, Peggy was making a doll's petticoat, Kitty and Grace were at play together. After a few minutes, during which nothing particular was said—

"You might as well finish that story, A. Z.," said Dick bluntly, turning round.

"Oh yes, that you might," said one or two more,

"It's so horrid wet," muttered Tom, "or else—grumble—grumble—grumble." It was quite impossible to say what the remainder of Tom's sentence was.

"I'll finish the story if you like, Dick," said A. Z.

And accordingly as soon as they had all settled where they would place themselves, she began :—

The giant now had all the world before him where to choose, but as he didn't know much about choosing, for it was all as yet pretty near the same to him, he thought the best thing to do would be simply to march straight forward. So he did that. He walked on for about a couple of hours, and then the trees began to get thinner, and at last they ceased altogether, and the giant got fairly out of the wood, and as far as he could see before him, and on either side of him, there was nothing but a great flat spread of land.

"I wonder if *this* is the world!" said the giant to himself. But he looked rather blank as he spoke, for he didn't care very much for the sort of thing. However, he thought he would go a little further before he made up his mind about it, so he first sat down on the grass, and ate up two or three of the loaves, and then he got on his legs again and began to march forward.

By the time he had walked for another hour or so, he liked the look of things rather better. He began to come upon a good many trees scattered here and there, which made him feel more comfortable, for, of course, until now, he had never so much as imagined a place without trees, and presently he even in the distance before him saw a cottage, which was so like the cottage in which he had always lived, that at first sight of it he shouted out "Hallo!" and fairly thought that he had got home again. However, he soon saw that that was a mistake, so he walked on quickly, and got to the door of the cottage, feeling a good deal of curiosity to know what sort of people might be living inside.

There was no knocker on the door he found when he reached it, so he rapped at it with his knuckles, and though he meant only to give a light little tap, yet the door quite shook when he knocked at it, and there was instantly such a screaming inside

THE GIANT'S SURPRISE.

Page 33.

that the giant couldn't think what on earth was the matter.

" Who's there ?" next moment roared out a very angry voice close to the keyhole.

" It's only me," answered the giant, in rather a frightened tone, and he was just beginning to think whether it wouldn't perhaps be best to turn and run, when suddenly the door was opened in his face, and if the people in the cottage had screamed loud before, they screamed ten times louder now, and, shrieking as if they would kill themselves, they tumbled over the chairs and tables, and bolted out at a back door, so that in less than a minute there wasn't a creature near the cottage but the giant himself. ·

Well, the giant had never been so astonished before in all the course of his life. " They must all be stark mad !" he thought, and for a little while he felt rather uncomfortable, and did not more than half like it ; but presently, as he was stooping down and peering into the cottage, he began to smell a very savoury smell, and putting his head right in, what should he see upon the table but a great dish of eggs and bacon, all smoking hot.

" Oh ho !" thought the giant, chuckling, " you were going to have your dinners, were you ? I'll just spare you the trouble of that." And in he went

D

on his hands and knees, and sat down on the floor,
and it was not long before he had emptied the dish.
He drank a great jug of beer, too, that he found
standing on the table, and when he had finished it
he felt ready for anything.

He did not care to stay in the cottage any longer,
so when his meal was finished he crept out at the
door again, and got up and went away. He was so
merry that he began to sing as he went along, trol-
ling out his song so loud that it was like the sound
of a waterfall. But after a little while he found a
very steep hill before him, and, as this tried his
breath, he had to leave off singing for a time while
he went up it.

As soon as ever he had got to the top, however,
he bethought him that he would begin to sing again;
so he did, and had just bellowed out his first words—

" There was a pretty maiden "——

when out there burst another scream louder than
anything he had heard yet, and something jumped
up before him, and then fell flat down upon the
ground.

Well, you may suppose that at that the giant
left off singing pretty quickly; in fact, he was so
startled by the dreadful noise that *he* screamed too,
and was very nearly tumbling down as well, when,

just as he was about to do so, he perceived that the person who had fallen first was nothing more nor less than a young girl. So, as soon as he saw that, he lost no time in recovering his senses. "Perhaps she's a princess!" he thought to himself, and his heart began to go pit-a-pat, and, thinking it was highly probable that she was, he went cautiously forward, and dropped upon his knees on the grass, and cleared his throat, and began to wonder what would be the best way of addressing her.

"Ahem! ahem!" coughed the giant; but, though he coughed so loud that all the echoes round began to say "Ahem!" too, yet the young woman at his side never moved so much as one of her eyelids.

"Dear me, what is the matter with her? Is she deaf?" thought the giant; and then he roared out, "Ahem!" again; and this time he made such a terrible noise that you would have thought a cannon had gone off, and the poor young woman started up from the ground, and in a moment had begun crying and screaming again as if her heart would break.

"Oh, don't kill me! don't kill me! I never did you any harm!" cried the young woman, and she flung her arms into the air, and hid her face on the ground, and conducted herself in so strange a way that the giant really did not know whatever to do.

"I don't want to kill you," said he, as soon as he

could manage to speak at all. "What on earth are
you screaming at?" And he was in such a rage
with her by this time that he took her by the arm
as he spoke, and shook her. But instead of that
quieting her, it made her give such a shriek that it
was like all the other shrieks she had given before
put into one, and in a moment more (for the noise
she made was so dreadful that, in his fright, the
giant, losing his hold of her, clapped both hands up
to his ears) she was scampering down the hill as
you never saw any one scamper in all your life.

"Why, _she's_ mad too!" cried the giant then,
and, as he stood on the hill top and watched her
pelting down, he almost wished he was back in the
cottage at home. For, you see, he had not in the
least begun to guess yet how it was because he was
a giant that people got in such a fright at sight of
him; he never had imagined such a thing as that,
and he was beginning to get quite uncomfortable at
the thought of having to live in such a mad world.
However, after pondering the matter in a very bad
temper for a little while, he remembered what his
father had said about not being in a hurry to come
back, and he made up his mind that he would try it
a little longer. So he began to go forward again.

He went down the hill by the same way that the
girl had gone, and presently, far away, at the bottom

of it, he saw a number of houses all built close to one another. "Oh ho!" thought the giant, "this must be a town;" and as he had never seen a town before he began to post towards it with all his might.

But while he was still some way from the bottom of the hill, he heard the most dreadful noises all at once coming from the houses that you can imagine, and in a moment more there was nothing to be seen but little black dots of people flying helter skelter in all directions.

"It must be a fire!" thought the giant at that, and he stood still, and for a moment almost thought of running away too; but then, though he looked with all his eyes, he could not anywhere see anything in the least degree like fire, or even like smoke; so, after scratching his head and considering the matter a little, he went forward again. But by the time he got to the town there was not a creature left in it. He went from street to street, and from house to house, and there was not a living soul in any one of them.

The giant was beginning to get a little used to strange things now, so he was not many minutes in making up his mind that he had better, without any delay, look about for a comfortable house to take up his quarters in. He looked into a good many, and at last he pitched upon the biggest one in the place, and having gone in there, and locked the door to keep out the family in case they should come back, he made himself at home in a very few minutes. He found a beautiful fire burning in the kitchen, and the tea things set, and the kettle boiling; so he sat down and had tea, and then, finding himself unusually sleepy—for he had taken a great deal more exercise during the day than he was at all used to—after nodding for half an hour, and nearly tumbling two or three times into the fire, he perceived that the best thing he could do would be to go to bed. So he fetched all the feather beds that there were in the house into the drawing room, and laid them on the floor there, and was asleep in five minutes.

He slept so soundly and so long that he never awoke next morning till it was quite late, and when he did open his eyes at last, he hardly knew whether the sun really had risen yet or not, for—what do you think?—all the windows were so blocked up by faces that scarcely a ray of daylight could come in. There they were—swarming up upon ladders and tables, and on one another's shoulders, all staring at him—two faces staring out of every pane—while he slept. You may fancy what a skurry there was the moment he began to move! Down they went pell-mell—over one another's heads—ladders and tables and all, and with such a dreadful noise, as they tumbled to the ground, that you would have thought the house itself was coming down. It startled the giant so that he bolted out of bed almost without knowing what he was doing, and in another moment he had thrown up the windows and had his head in the street.

"What's the matter?" cried the giant.

"Oh-h-h!" roared the people. And away they scudded as if they were mad.

"Stop! Hy!" called the giant.

But the louder he called they only ran the faster.

"It's a most extraordinary thing!" said the giant.

However he was too hungry just then to trouble himself much about it, so he went away down-stairs and poked up the kitchen fire, and made a fine breakfast upon a leg of mutton and a cold goose which he found in the larder.

He was too busy, as long as he went on eating, to think much more of what was going on outside; but when his meal was finished he thought he would go upstairs again and take another look out at the window. And accordingly up he went, and as soon as he got near the window he saw that all the people had come back again, and had filled the street, so thick that you could hardly have thrown an apple between them; and when he put out his head and stared at them, though they all began to shake so that they could scarcely stand, yet this time they did not run away.

When he saw that, the giant began to laugh.

"Ho! ho! ho!" laughed the giant; and he nearly blew two or three of the people away, he laughed so loud.

"Oh don't!—don't!" cried the people, when they saw what he was doing.

"Don't *what*?" roared the giant.

"Don't laugh so loud!" cried the people.

But the giant only laughed at that louder than ever, so that the noise he made broke nearly all the windows in the street, and put the people in such a fright that full half of them ran away.

"What *are* you running away for now?" cried the giant.

"The glass is flying all over our heads!" cried the people.

"Why, dear me, so it is," said the giant; and he looked up and down the street quite amazed, for he had not an idea that *he* had broken the windows.

"Oh, pray don't laugh again! We'll do anything if you'll be quiet! We'll bring you as much food as you can eat!" shouted the people.

"That's very kind of you," answered the giant. "Suppose you go and bring it then." And he had scarcely spoken, when off a dozen or two of them pelted as hard as they could run.

Then the giant sat down by the window, and began quite condescendingly to talk to the people.

"I've come out to see the world," said the giant.

"Oh!—to see the world, have you?" said the people.

"Yes, to see the world, and—oh, by the way," said the giant, just remembering it, "you haven't such a thing as a princess here, have you?"

"A princess!" echoed the people, and they all turned as white as sheets with fright. "No!"

"Oh!—well, it isn't much matter. But I'm looking for one," said the giant.

"We have some delicious young lambs,—or if you could fancy a fat calf or two"—— said the people, all shaking in their shoes.

But when they had got so far, the giant burst into such a fresh roar of laughter that all the people together had to thrust their fingers into their ears, and could not utter another word.

"Lambs!" cried the giant. "Ho! ho!—lambs and fat calves! Ho! ho! ho!" And he had fairly to hold his sides with laughter. "Don't you know the difference between a princess, and a—ho! ho! ho!—a lamb and a fat calf?"

Well, yes, of course, the people tried to tell him

they did know the difference between the things he
mentioned; but they had ventured to hope—and then
they all began to shake again—that, as they had not
got a princess in the place at all, the giant might
possibly condescend to be satisfied with the flavour
of a tender young calf.

But they had hardly got the words out of their
mouths when the giant was roaring louder than ever,
and rolling backwards and forwards—he was in such
a state of glee.

"They think I want to *eat* her!" cried the giant.
"Oh! oh!—they think I want to eat her!" And
it was several minutes before he could sit upright
again.

Of course the people in the street felt a good
deal comforted when they saw how much amused at
that notion the giant was.

"I want to *marry* her!" said the giant, as soon
as he could speak.

"Oh!—to marry her, do you?" echoed the
people; and, hard as they had been staring at him
before, they all stared harder than ever now.

"Yes," said the giant, "that's the chief reason
why I'm here."

And upon that all the people together gave such
a sigh of relief that it was like a great wind in the
place.

"Now," said the giant confidentially, looking down over the window, "if any of you know where I could find such a thing—because I'm rather in a hurry—I wish you'd tell me. You know what a princess is like?—glittering all over, you know—like one of the stars," said the giant, remembering the description his father had given him.

But the people only stared in his face at this, and though one and all opened their mouths, they never so much as uttered a word.

"Did you never see one?" roared the giant then, beginning to get in a rage.

"No-o-o!" said the people, all turning as white again as ghosts.

"Then you're a pack of fools!" said the giant in a fury; and he drew in his head, and was just going to dash down the casement, when all the people in the street began to make such a piteous howling that he could not help, out of pure curiosity, looking out again to see what was the matter with them.

"Oh, have pity on us! Don't kill us! Have mercy on us, and we'll do whatever you ask!" howled the people.

Then the giant forgot all about his anger, and burst out laughing again, for he was beginning at last to see how the matter stood, and I can tell you he felt not a little vain at discovering what a terrible fellow he was thought to be.

"Well, I 'll think about it," said the giant, as soon as he could compose himself. And he tried to look very severe, and frowned, and shook his head. "I 'll think about it," he said.

And at that the people cried—"Oh, thank you, Giant! Thank you!" And you would have thought to hear them that the giant was the kindest friend they had on earth.

So in a few minutes more they had made a compact together that if the people would supply the giant with everything he wanted, he would not just at present take their lives. And then the people went away quite happy, and the giant went downstairs to have his lunch.

Now (said A. Z.) I must leave you to imagine very much for yourselves the sort of life that the giant led for a good while after this. He lived in this big house like a king in his palace, and all the people in the town were as his servants. From morning till night he did nothing but think of what he should most like to have, and call out for it, and as soon as ever he called a score of people would run to bring the thing he called for. It was a very royal life.

But still, after it had lasted for some time, the giant began to get a little tired of it.

"I may as well go and see something new," said the giant to himself; "I was born to be king of all the world,"—this was the way in which the giant had come to talk of himself now,—"so it's hardly fit that I should go on wasting time here. They're very well-meaning people, but it's hardly, after all, the sort of place for *me*."

So one morning the giant looked out at the window, and called—"Hy!" At which all the people came running together pell-mell.

"I called you here," said the giant, when they were all assembled, "just to say to you that I'm going away."

"Going away!" echoed the people, and though they could almost have leaped into the air for joy, yet they were in such fear of the giant, that they all made their faces half a yard long.

"Yes," said the giant, "I'm going. I ought to see a little more of the world. I *may* perhaps come back again some day,"—they all began to shake like aspen leaves when he said that,—"but for the present, I'm going. So fetch me a good bag of provisions, and I'll say good bye to you."

You may be sure they fetched him the provisions even quicker than they had ever fetched him anything yet, and as soon as they had brought the bag, he threw it on his back and nodded good-bye to them, and went off.

For a long time after this the giant wandered about, now staying in one place, now in another, and wherever he went he had everything pretty much his own way. No matter where it was, all the people fell on their knees before him, or, if they did not, he soon made them; he had nothing to do but to knock down a dozen or two of them, and the rest were sure after that to come to their senses. So the giant soon came to think that the world was an extremely pleasant place to live in.

After this had gone on for a long time, and the giant had grown so haughty and exacting and tyrannical that what to do with him the poor people who had to entertain him scarcely knew, and all the country round was filled with groans and sighs because of him, one day he left a town in which he had been staying, ruining everybody in the place with the fine entertainments he had made them give him for a month or two; and, as he was going along, wondering what he should come to next (for, though he had everything he asked for, he was continually giving prodigious yawns, and longing for something new), he presently came upon a man on horseback riding softly towards him.

"Hallo!" thought the giant to himself, "who have we got here?" And he pricked up his ears, and marched forward briskly, for he had not seen a creature for three or four hours, and was beginning to feel quite tired of being alone.

So, as soon as he came near to him—

" Halt! " cried the giant.

Upon which the horseman halted at once—horse and man quite quietly—and stood looking at the giant as if he was not a bit bigger than himself.

" Ahem! " said the giant, a little confounded at that, and clearing his throat—" Ahem! Who are you ? "

" Who are you who ask me ? " answered the horseman.

Upon which in an instant the giant flew into a rage.

" Who am I ? I 'll teach you to know who I am! " roared the giant; and he flung up his arm to give him such a box on the ears as should send him to the ground; when in an instant it seemed as if the sun flashed out before him, and next moment not the horseman but the giant himself lay on the earth.

" Not a strong arm that of yours, Giant," the horseman said quietly. And the giant, when he tried to raise himself, found he was so weak that he could not so much as clamber up upon his knees.

You may fancy to yourselves the rage the giant was in then. He was in such a state that he foamed at the mouth.

"You're a magician!—your're a wizard!—you're an evil spirit!" roared the giant, plunging about to try and get on his feet, with the beads of perspiration standing on his forehead with passion and fright.

But the horseman only said—"Hush, poor fool!" And after a minute he stooped and took the giant's hand in his, and, as if he had been a child, lifted him up. At that the giant's tongue clove to the roof of his mouth, and he trembled like an old man as he stood.

Then the horseman took a part of his horse's reins, and flung them over the giant's neck, and said—"Follow me;" and began to ride forward. And, though the giant tried to tear off the rein, yet, lightly as it had been thrown, it seemed to clasp him round like an iron chain, and the horse dragged him forward, and, would he or would he not, he had to follow where the rider went.

The rider rode on softly towards a hill that lay before him, on the top of which, rising out of a crest of trees, stood a great castle, with towers and turrets springing up into the sky, all glittering in the sun like gold.

"It looks like a king's palace," thought the giant; and in the midst of his shame and rage and consternation his mouth watered to get possession of it. "If I could only get this rein off me," he thought to himself, and in his fury he threw himself down upon the ground again, and dug his teeth into the rein, and tried to gnaw it through, and howled so that you would have thought the place was full of wild beasts. But he could no more cut the rein asunder than if it had been made of rings of steel.

"Rise up!" cried the horseman then; and, though he had spoken quite quietly before, this time his voice rang out like a trumpet, and he struck the spurs into his horse, and the beast rushed up the hill, and once more the giant had to get on his legs, and, would he or would he not, again to follow at the horse's heels.

So in that manner, without another word, they went up the hill, and got to the castle gate, and when they arrived there the horseman took a little bugle from his side, and blew a note, and immediately the castle doors flew open, and the giant found himself in a great court paved with marble, and all the walls around him, and the castle in the middle of them, were built of marble too, and the towers and turrets of the castle were of gold. Anything so splendid the giant had never seen in all his life before, and as he looked at it he roared and gnashed his very teeth for fury.

The horseman rode into the middle of the court, the giant following after him; then he sprang from his horse, and in the same moment lifted off the rein

E

from the giant's neck—upon which, as you may suppose, the vicious giant made another spring at him,
but the horseman with a laugh merely caught his arm,
and the giant could no more lift it again than if he
had been a child of a week old.

Then the horseman said once more—"Follow
me;" and he went in at the palace door, and the
giant, without power to resist, went after him.

They went into a large kingly hall, all glittering
with gold and jewels. There were no windows in it,
yet—though in what way the giant could not tell—
the light entered into it, a light softer than sunlight.
There were a great many people in the hall, and
when the horseman entered they all bowed low before
him, and made a way for him to walk up through
the centre of it, which he did, the giant following
still at his heels, till he reached the far end. Then
he stood still, and said to the giant—

"Lie down."

"Where?" asked the giant sullenly.

"Here," answered the horseman, and he pointed
to the floor at the head of the hall.

So the giant, foaming at the mouth, lay down,
and he lay between the two side walls of the hall,
his head touching the one and his feet the other.

Then the horseman raised his voice, and said—
"Bring a net and cover him!" and half a dozen

people ran and brought a net and threw it over him. It was a net so large that it covered him from head to foot, and the meshes of it were made of steel. The poor giant gave a great howl, and began to kick for his life when they threw it over him, but in a moment they had it fastened down to the floor with iron skewers, and the giant was as helpless under it as though he lay at the bottom of the sea.

As soon as he saw that it was all over with him, he began to make such a noise that you might have heard him half a dozen miles away. He howled so loud, and roared out such wicked words, that all the people in the hall stopped their ears, and half of them in a fright ran away—which, as soon as he saw it, only made the giant howl louder than ever; in fact, he exerted himself out of spite to such an extent that he got quite black in the face, as if he was going to have a fit. And he probably would have had one if they had let him go on much longer, but, just as he was getting together all his breath to give one more horrid howl than any that had gone before, the horseman called out—" Gag him ! " and in a moment the net was lifted from his face and a gag was in his mouth, and the great howl was stopped for ever. Then, after that, you could only see by the look in his eyes that the giant was almost out of his mind with fury.

He lay and looked into the horseman's face, and the horseman stood and looked at him. The horseman had thrown off his riding hat and cloak now, and though his clothes were dark and plain, he had a gold crown set on his golden hair, and the giant knew that he was a king.

So, when they had both looked at one another for a minute or more—

"So thou thoughtest," said the king, "that my dominion was thine,—thou thoughtest that *thou* wert fit to be a king!" And then he looked at him with a very pitying smile, and said—"Thou poor fool! Lie there and learn what a king's life is."

And when he had said these words he turned away, and instead of *his* face—which, though it was grave, was so beautiful that it was like an angel's— crowds and crowds of other faces came, and looked at the giant, and mocked or pitied him. And so it went on all day, and the giant's staring, burning eyeballs never stopped glaring at them all till night came, and the hall at last was left empty.

Night and day the giant lay under the net for weeks and weeks. Nobody took much notice of him; after the first day or two nearly all the people went to and fro without almost looking at him. Once every morning, for the first week or so, the king came and stood beside him, and as soon as he came some one raised the net, and took the gag out of the giant's mouth, and then the king said—

" Wilt thou lie silent, Giant ? "

But the giant always in answer to that question gave only a vicious howl; and in a moment more the gag was clapped on him again, and the net was fastened down, and the king went away.

Till at last one day when the king came as usual and asked—" Wilt thou be silent ? " the giant, instead of his usual howl, uttered never a sound.

So that day there was a pause after the king had spoken; and then he said—" Let down the net." And the net was fastened down, but the giant's mouth was free. But after that day, for a long time, the king did not come to his side again.

After a little while, when the giant's first rage was partly over (for you know, however badly we are treated, even the best of us can't live in a downright rage for ever), he began to look about him, and to find that a great deal that was very curious went on in the great hall. It was a busy place; and the strangest thing was that the busiest person in it seemed to be the king. Other people's work began and ended, but *his* work seemed to be for ever. Rest for others : no rest for him.

" The man must be out of his wits ! " thought the giant to himself again and again.

No rest for him. Whoever had pain, or sorrow, or trouble, came and laid down his burden before *him*. Sometimes the king could heal the trouble at once, and he who had suffered from it went away blessing the king's name; sometimes it took days of patient work to get it healed; but, let the time required be long or short, the king refused it to no one—turned no one away. There were people of every sort that came to him—rich men clothed in embroidered robes, and poor men and women dressed in sorrowful rags; but, never heeding their rich clothes or their tattered coats, the king gave to them all alike, or, if he favoured any, it was always, as the giant saw with wonder, those who were the poorest clad amongst them—the oldest and feeblest, men weighed down with age and sorrow, women white-faced with want, little children (for even children came to him) with naked feet. And, let what tales there would be told to him, so that they were sad and true, he let no one go from him without comfort. Only they *must* be true; that was a necessity, the giant saw. If the stories were false, then the tellers of them were swept out from the king's presence, and they went away scorned and despised of all people.

A great many days had passed since the gag had been taken out of the giant's mouth (though no one had yet said a word to him, nor he to any one), when one day again the king, as he came into the hall, stopped by the side of the net, and looked at the giant, and said—

"Art thou learning thy lesson, Giant?"

But the giant made no answer, and the king passed on.

Yet after that, each morning as he came first into the hall, the king stopped at the giant's side, and asked—

"Art thou learning thy lesson?"

And generally the giant scowled and said nothing; and once or twice he said sullenly—

"I am learning *no* lesson!"

But when he said that he told a lie—for he was. He did not want to learn it, and fought against learning it with all his might, but learn it he did, for he could not help himself. Day after day he learnt what it was to be a king.

He used to lie under his net, and find himself listening with the strangest kind of interest to the stories that were told the king. "I daresay they're all a pack of lies!" he used to mutter to himself every now and then, and, if anybody came near him and seemed to look at him, he would pretend to be whistling, or would begin to twirl his thumbs, or what you please—but in half a minute you may be sure he was stretching his ears again to hear every word that was being said—wondering, too, all the time what the king would do at the end, and how he would set all that was so wrong right.

"If I were he I'd do—this or that," he used to find himself muttering sometimes; and when by chance it turned out that the king perhaps *did* do just what the giant thought that *he* would have done in his place, the giant could have bellowed out for satisfaction. He once or twice did almost call out—"Bravo!" and only stopped himself by pretending that he had got a frightful cough when the word was half out of his mouth.

But of course after anything of this sort he was always dreadfully ashamed of himself, for the giant thought it was very weak and foolish indeed to take an interest in anybody's business except his own,— and indeed he never had been guilty of such a thing in all his life before. But still they *were* such curious stories that were told the king, that really for the life of him he could not help listening to them. So, if he was ashamed of himself to-day, he was listening as hard as ever again to-morrow. And, which was curious, the more he listened the more he desired to hear, and strange thoughts would come at times into the giant's mind,—so that sometimes he would even forget altogether about himself, and how ill-used he was, lying there under his net like a miserable imprisoned fish, and would begin instead to ponder wonderingly about the things that this king did; and day by day this grew upon him, till at last the strangest feeling came to him—a sort of bewitchment he thought it was—which made him watch the king morning and noon and night, and listen for his voice, and catch the sound of it among all other voices there, and when each dawn came kept him counting hours and minutes till the king should come for that one daily moment to his side. A feeling that seemed to force him to do things he never meant to do; for one day, after a long time, when the king came and looked at him, and said as usual—"Art thou learning thy lesson, Giant?" the giant neither held his tongue, nor growled out as before—"I am learning *no* lesson!" but slowly answered—"Yes."

That day the king remained standing by him, and the giant and the king each looked in the other's face for a long time, and then the king said softly—

"Have patience a little longer."

And, having said that, he went away. And the giant lay still, and uttered never a word more, but all day long he watched the king as he moved here and there, rolling his big eyes after him wherever he went, and a great solemn fear of him came into his heart, the like of which he had never felt in all his life before; and he listened as he had never listened yet when the old and the poor came in to tell their stories to the king, and as he heard them strange feelings stirred about the giant's heart, and strange mists came into his eyes.

For this was the truth, that the giant—the lazy, selfish, brutish giant—had looked on the bright face with its golden hair till it seemed to him now more beautiful than all the palace that it lived in, and had hearkened to the silver voice till the words it uttered had come to sound in his great mule's ears like music. There he lay imprisoned under his net, and all this day, instead of thinking to himself, "Oh, what a noble, ill-used giant I am!" and gnashing his teeth, and longing to have his fingers about everybody's throat, he was muttering over and over again—"Oh, what a brute beast I am!" and ever so much more in the same style, the like of which, I think, never entered before into a big, idle, worthless giant's head.

But the giant lay very still, and never uttered a word aloud to any one all day; and, during that day, and during several days that followed, the king almost seemed to have forgotten that the giant lay there at all, for he came, and went, and never spoke to him, and morning and night the giant watched and watched for him in vain, and grew all in a tremble fifty times a day, when he thought that he was coming near him, and all to no end, for look as he might the king never came.

Until at last one day very early in the morning, when the giant lay awake, watching the light of the sunrise as it floated in through the great room, and thinking how the splendour of it on the walls was like the gold of the king's hair—in that hour, very quietly, the king came in alone, and the giant looked up and saw him standing by his side; but the sunlight fell so full all round him that the giant had to shade his eyes for a few moments before he could look at the bright face and the burning hair.

"Is the lesson learnt, Giant?" said the king.

And the giant humbly answered—

"Yes."

Then the king stooped down, and looked him very sharply in the face, and asked him—

"Wilt thou have thy liberty?"

To which, trembling, the giant answered, "Yes," again.

And then the king pulled out the iron skewers, and lifted up the net, and said—

"I give thee back what I took from thee. Rise up."

And the giant rose up, but only for a moment, and then in a great tremble fell down at the king's feet.

"Art thou conquered, Giant?" said the king softly.

"I am thy servant!" the giant said, and fell into a great burst of weeping.

The king laid his hand on the giant's head, tenderly, as if he was touching a child.

"Not by force nor by injustice," he said solemnly, " but by love and by mercy shalt thou ever be great and honoured on the earth. Thy strength and thy might are thine not to destroy, but to succour, not to crush, but to uphold. Thou hast learnt this. Rise now, and go thy way."

"No; no!—let me stay with thee!" cried the giant.

But the king said softly—

"Not now. Another time thou shalt return to me,—but thou must go now."

"Where shall I go?" asked the giant.

"Home!" said the king.

Then the giant kissed his feet, and rose up,— and home he went.

———

Having got to which point A. Z. paused, and shut her mouth.

"But that isn't the end, A. Z.?" cried Dick, firing up under a sense of imposition.

"Yes; it is the end," said A. Z.

"But it isn't an end at all!" said contemptuous Tom.

"It's as good an end as you need have. What else do you want?" asked A. Z. "The story can't go on for ever."

"No—but *did* he go home, A. Z.?" asked Kitty.

"Yes, Kitty," said A. Z. "I told you he did."

"And was he good?" inquired Peggy (who, being herself the best behaved of all the six, was always very much interested about the faults of other people).

"Yes; the best giant from that time forward that ever lived," answered A. Z.

"Oh!" returned Peggy, slightly disappointed.

"And, A. Z.," said Frank with the great grey eyes, "did he ever go back and live with the king?"

"Yes," said A. Z., "after a long time, when his father and mother were dead, then he went back. And he never left the king again, but lived with him to the end of his life."

"And did he marry the king's daughter?" cried little Gracie.

"Well, Gracie, now you remind me of it," said A. Z., "to be sure he did!"

"And so he got a princess after all!" said Peggy

softly, thinking with satisfaction of how virtue was rewarded.

"And was *she* a giantess?" asked Tom.

"No, Tom; not to begin with," answered A. Z., "but she grew so fast after she married the giant that in the course of a year or two she was quite as big as he was."

"Oh!" cried Gracie, who had believed so much that she was running over now, and could not take in another word.

Seeing which, A. Z. laughed, and, rising up, put away her work.

"Do you never tell stories about real people, A. Z.?" asked Tom, about the middle of dinner next day, after he had taken off the first fine edge of his appetite.

"Oh, yes," answered A. Z.; "often. What real person do you want a story about?"

"I don't want a story about anybody in particular," replied Tom; "but I mean, can't you tell something about people like *us—real* people, you know. I don't care about giants and that sort of stuff," said practical Tom.

But there was rather an uproar at the table when Tom had expressed this sentiment, and it appeared that the children generally did not at all agree with Tom—or with one another.

"Giants are far nicer than fairies," said Dick, who, being a big strong boy, took a sort of brotherly interest in giants.

"Oh no, Dick! I like fairies best!" cried Gracie, who was like a fairy herself.

"I like ghosts," said Kitty, who had a great appetite for the terrible and marvellous (but who was such a sensible, brave little woman, that all the ghosts in the world wouldn't have made a coward of her).

"There are no such things as ghosts!" cried scornful Tom.

"I don't like ghost stories," said Peggy. "I don't think they're right."

At which everybody laughed, for the speech was so like Peggy. Peggy herself, however, of course didn't laugh, but looked as grave as a judge.

"I like fairy stories, but I think I like true stories best," said Frank, speaking last, as he often did. "I like stories about great people. Do you know any like that, A. Z. ?"

But upon this the other children began to clamour again.

"Oh, that would be something stupid, Frankie!" cried Grace.

"Unless it was about a soldier; and I don't think you could tell a story about a soldier properly," said blunt Tom.

"I think your head's turned about soldiering, Tom," said Peggy severely. "A. Z., isn't it wicked to be a soldier?"

"Oh, you goose!" shouted Dick.

"Children," said A. Z., "if I should try to please you all, I see I should end by pleasing none of you. So I'll choose a story for myself, and if anybody likes it, well and good. I'll tell you a story about a shepherd boy."

"A shepherd boy!" echoed Tom. "That's about as stupid as a giant."

"A shepherd boy doesn't necessarily mean nothing but a shepherd, Tom," answered A. Z. "King David was a shepherd boy once."

At which Tom had nothing more to say. So when dinner was over they all went into the parlour, and A. Z. told them this tale.

STORY THE SECOND.

THE SHEPHERD-BOY.

MY shepherd-boy [said A. Z.] lived in Italy, at a place with a long name— Vespignano, it was called, but you need not remember it unless you like; you need only remember that it was in the north of Italy, near to Florence and the Apennine Mountains. He was the son of a shepherd called Bondoné, and, as his own christian name was a very long one too, we will just call him "Little Bondoné"—as I daresay he really *was* often called when he was a lad.

Now Bondoné the father—Big Bondoné—was quite a poor man; shepherds generally are, you know, and especially in those times (for this was all long ago) poor working people had to live in a very hard way indeed. There was plenty of work

F

to be done, and not much pay to be got for it, so that even those who liked to work had often a hard time of it (as too many people have still), and those who were idle and did not like to work (a very strange sort of people *they* must have been ; you can scarcely form an idea of them—can you, Dick and Tom ?)—had a hard business sometimes to keep from starving.   But still these idle ones were such *very* strange people that I have heard they would rather live half starved, if they might but lie out in the streets all day in the sunshine, than have enough to eat by working for it.   Bondoné, however, was not one of that sort.   As far as I know he worked very hard, and did the best he could to support himself and his wife and his little son like respectable people, and as soon as his little son was old enough to be turned to any use, he set *him* to work too.

He set him to work to watch the sheep.   It does not need a boy to be very big, you know, to do that. A little boy and a good dog can keep a good many sheep in order.—that is, if he keeps wide awake, and has his wits about him.   But I am obliged to confess that I can't help doubting very much if little Bondoné made a good shepherd boy ; I can't help thinking that unless his dog happened to have been a very good dog indeed—not only a so-so dog, who wanted driving, and directing, and keeping up to his duty, but a really clever wide-awake dog—he must have got sometimes, up there on the mountains with his sheep, into a very pretty pickle.

For the truth was, that the little boy's heart was by no means given to shepherding. Sheep themselves he liked, but to be running after sheep, and watching sheep, and thinking of sheep from morning to night, was what he had not the slightest taste for at all. I can fancy him in the chill early mornings driving his sheep up to their pasturage—not dreamily then, I daresay, for he was a fine healthy boy, and loved a good race round a field, I have little doubt, as well as anybody. I can fancy him driving them to their appointed place, and then sitting down on the hill side, and presently—slowly and slowly—forgetting everything about them—beginning to think of quite other things than sheep; looking up to the fair hills all round him, and thinking sweet and solemn things about them; lying on his back upon the grass perhaps, and looking up to the sky over- head, and tracing out strange shapes in the changes of its wonderful clouds; lying upon his breast on some green bank, and seeing even in the grass and wild flowers over it more than ever shepherd boy's eyes had seen in grass and flowers before.

"Dreaming away from morning to night," I dare- say his father would often say with a groan. "Dream-

ing and drawing images. Ugh! The boy will come
to no good in this world!"

Drawing — yes, that was the thing that little
Bondoné loved—that was what his heart was set on.
Morning, noon, and night he would be drawing.
Not as *you* draw, Frank [said A. Z.] with pencil and
paper; little Bondoné had never possessed a sheet
of paper in his life, and as to a lead pencil, he
had never so much as seen such a thing. No, his
paper was a bit of clear wall, a flat stone when he
could find one, a piece of slate, the ground itself
when there was nothing better, and his pencil was a
lump of chalk, or a sharp flint, or sometimes, perhaps,
the black end of a burnt stick. *He* knew very little
indeed about black lead and drawing-paper.

Yet with only such a pencil as he could get he
drew almost everywhere. I can fancy how he made
drawings in the cottage at home, inside and out, till
there was not a clear spot of it left. There would
be half a dozen portraits of his father, with his shepherd's coat and stick, and his mother's likeness, I am
sure, ten times over, and here would be the good
shepherd dog, barking and running at the sheep, and
here and there and everywhere, I am very certain,
there must have been the sheep themselves.

"There never was so clever a boy!" the good
mother must often have said proudly to herself, as

she looked at them all, and saw how really they
were so like to living men and women and dogs and
sheep that a very child might know what they were
meant for ; and though Bondoné the father might
always pooh-pooh the whole thing, and tell his son
fifty times over that he had a mind to pitch his
lumps of chalk and burnt stick into the fire, yet I
can't but suspect that even he sometimes, and not so
seldom either, would cast a glance or two at the
cottage walls, and give a grim smile at the way the
boy had caught his look, or fixed the glance of his
mother's eye.

As for the lad himself, he did not think much of
any of these pictures ; I doubt if he would have got
to think much of them if all the people in Vespignano had said how fine they were—for he knew that
they were not fine—not what *he* called fine at all ;
and he had even already in his head and heart the
thoughts of other pictures, by the side of which
these on the cottage walls would look poor indeed.
So he left his father and his mother to think what
they liked of these, little heeding what they said,
and he himself would lie on the hill side with his
sheep, and, gazing on the hills, with their wild shapes
and changing shadows, and on the sunshine lighting
far away the windings of the silver river, and on the
colours of the clouds of heaven, would stretch his

arms out to the sky, and cry from the very bottom of his heart—" Oh, that I might live to be a painter!"

But he was a shepherd-boy and no painter, and perhaps—we cannot tell—he might have gone on tending sheep all his life long if it had not happened that one day when he sat as usual on the hills, a stranger walking that way chanced to see him. He was sitting with a piece of slate on his knees and a sharp stone, and was hard at work. One of the sheep had lain down on the grass near to him, and had gone to sleep, and little Bondoné was fast setting the likeness of him on the slate. He had drawn many a sheep, you know, before now, so he went at this one quickly, and had him taken in a few minutes—head and tail and wool and all. So then it was, as he was putting the last touches to him, that the stranger came passing by, and, being sharp-sighted, and seeing at a little distance something of what was going on, came quietly nearer, and looked down over the boy's head.

" What's this you're doing ? Who taught you to draw sheep, my boy ? " said the stranger, looking at the slate.

" Nobody taught me, sir," answered the lad.

" What, nobody ? How did you learn then ? " the stranger asked.

THE SHEPHERD BOY AND THE STRANGER.

Page 70.

"Only by looking at the sheep, sir," answered little Bondoné.

At which the stranger smiled (for even in those days there were people who, when they drew sheep, or anything else, seemed quite to forget that it was a good thing to look at them), and—

"Give me your slate," he said.

So Bondoné stood up and gave it, and the stranger took the slate and looked at little Bondoné's drawing for full five minutes without speaking ever a word. Then he lifted up his head, and said,—"Come here." And he began, as the boy stood by his side, to point out faults in the little drawing—one fault after another, sharply and clearly, and the lad listened, with his cheeks burning and his heart beginning to beat hard, for as the stranger talked to him he felt that he must be a painter.

At last the stranger put the slate aside, and looked into the boy's face steadily, and said to him—

"Should you like to learn to draw?"

"Yes, sir," the boy answered, "with all my heart."

"If you were able to draw what would you do?"

"I would go to Florence," answered the boy, colouring hotter than ever, "and try to be a painter —like Cimabué." For Cimabué was the name of the greatest painter who was then living in Italy.

"What do you know about Cimabué?" said the stranger. "What can you, living here on the mountains, have ever heard of him?"

Then the lad smiled softly to himself, and answered—

"My father took me once to Florence, and as we walked in the streets we saw a great procession coming to us carrying a picture that they were going to set over an altar in a church, and all the city was making holiday because of it. It was a picture of Cimabué's. I saw it, sir, when they had put it in the church. It was a Madonna." And the lad's voice went low as he said that, for he had spent hours and hours since then over the thought of that Madonna.

"And so *you* want to be a painter, too, like that one," the stranger said, after they had both been silent for a moment, "and to make men's hearts glad with the sight of your work? But, my boy, to be a painter is no easy task. Those who make themselves such work hard for many years—nay, they never cease from working. A true painter only ceases to learn when he ceases to live."

"Yes, sir," the boy answered, colouring deeply; "but that is his glory."

"Yes, it is his glory, if he *be* true," the stranger answered sadly. "But do you know how many are that? Only one here and there. My lad, there is many a one ready to put his hand to the plough, but few who do not grow weary of their work before the sun sets."

Year after year had the boy tended sheep upon the hills, but never yet had a day come to him like this one. Long after the stranger had left him and gone away, I can fancy how he seemed to see a new light in the heavens, and a new glory over the mountain-side. How he must have dreamed that afternoon away! What strange, bright castles in the air he must have built! He had built many a castle before this, lying and looking into the sky till he had pretty nigh forgotten all that made his life upon the earth, but to-day, for the first time, these castles of his had got as it were a foot to stand on. They were not *all* air and mist—bright clouds that would fade away when he rose up like the vapours from the hills.

The stranger had said before he went that they might perhaps meet again. How the lad must have pondered over these words, and built all sorts of hopes upon them. Would the stranger really come again? What did good shepherd-dog Fido think? I daresay when the daylight began to fade, and little Bondoné had driven his sheep into their fold, and was trudging home with Fido by his side, he asked

the dog that question half a dozen times. Now
what *did* Fido think? Would anything come of
it? Fido—wise dog!—must also have had his own
thoughts.

The lad was longing to tell his mother what had
happened. He was so happy that he wanted her to
be glad with him. As soon as ever he had got into
the house he told his story to her—to her and to his
father too, for they were both there. Perhaps, as he
told it, all breathless with eagerness, he never saw
the sadness in his mother's face, nor wondered that
they shewed so little surprise at his tale. Perhaps
he saw nothing unusual in the look of either of them
until, when he paused at last for breath, his father
startled him by saying this:

"If the stranger had said to you—'Will you
come with me?' what would you have said to him,
my son?"

Then you may think how the boy opened his
eyes wide, and how the colour rushed into his face.

"Father, why do you ask me that? What do
you mean?" he said.

"He has asked *me* the question—that is all, my
boy," the father answered.

And then the mother said in her sad voice—

"He came and looked at all your drawings—at
all the pictures you have made of your father and of

me, my dear; and he said, if you liked to go with him he would make a painter of you. But, oh my son," cried the poor mother, "you won't go away and leave me?"

She went to the lad, and laid her arm about his neck and kissed him; but when she looked into his face after her kiss, her heart sank.

"Mother, I *must* go," the boy said. He went away from her, and sat down: he couldn't speak for some moments.

"Ay, lad, you will go," the father said; "I knew that. I said to him I would give him no answer, either yea or nay, until to-morrow; but I might have answered him yea without thinking twice about it. What! not a word, boy? Are you thinking of that morning we saw his picture in the streets at Florence? I made him smile when I told him what a mad lad you were that day. He said"—

"Father, what are you talking of? *Who* said?" the boy cried out. He had leaped to his feet, his face all burning.

"He—Cimabué," the father answered. "It was he, my son."

"*He* who spoke to me on the hill? *He* who has asked to teach me, father?"

"Yes, lad," said the father quietly; "even he."

The room was quite still after the father had said

those last words. The first sound that broke the silence presently was one cry, " Oh, mother, let me go !" as the boy threw himself into his mother's arms.

So they let him go. He had kept his last watch on the hills. The next day, when the great painter came again, they let the lad go home with him to Florence.

Frank [said A. Z., addressing herself to Frank especially, for, to tell the truth, he only of all the children seemed to be paying much attention to this story. Dick and Tom had fairly begun a game of noughts and crosses on Tom's slate, and Kitty and Gracie were rolling together with audible satisfaction on the sofa. Peggy, indeed, was preserving a respectable outward appearance of attention ; but, then, Peggy had a way of *always* looking attentive, which, though it put, as it were, a good face upon a thing, was not quite to be looked upon as a conclusive sign of her enjoyment of it. So A. Z., finding Frank's grey eyes the only ones that were fixed upon her face, addressed her next words to him.

Frank, she said—] you will read the rest of Bondoné's story some day for yourself—told far better than I could tell it to you. I don't know enough about painters and painters' studios to describe to you how he set to work when he got to Florence. I only know he *did* work, hard and well. Cimabué had other pupils besides him, but none of them worked as he did. And Cimabué cared for none of them as he cared for him.

Well and steadily, month after month, and year after year, the lad worked. I think he often went back to the old home at Vespignano, and made the father and mother there glad with a sight of him. I daresay he often walked over the hills where he had sat as a little lad tending his sheep, and thought of many things as he trod them. Do you think the father and mother were not proud of him? When perhaps he brought them up to Florence, and shewed them the pictures he had painted, I can imagine how their hearts must have swelled, and when they heard men speak in praise of him, how the happy colour must have come into their checks.

I do not know if *all* men are born for one especial purpose, but the *greatest* men are. Perhaps one might have made many things of this boy Bondoné, but God had made him for one thing above all others, and so he clung to that; and became in it, for as long as he lived, the first man in Italy, and in all the world. There have been greater painters since, Frank, but *he* led the way for those who followed: none before him had ever been so great as he. Not Cimabué: for there came a day when even he, who had taught him—loving his art, like a true painter, more than himself or his own glory—came and bowed his head before the shepherd-boy.

He painted pictures in many cities, but he left his best to Florence : you may see them there now. He left something to Florence, too, beyond pictures. He could build as well as paint, and he set within its walls the fairest tower that there is in all Italy—a bell-tower—Campanile, they call it—which has been the delight of men who love these things for more than five hundred years. You may go to Florence, Frank, and see that too.

He painted pictures for forty years, and then he died. The old father and mother at Vespignano must have been dead long before that. It was very long ago, Frank—five hundred years ago and more ; but, in spite of all the great painters who have lived and worked since, the world has not yet forgotten the name of that shepherd-boy.

———⤞•••⤝———

" But, A. Z.!"—said Frank, opening his eyes wide.

The game of noughts and crosses had for a few moments been suspended, while Tom gave his mind in some amazement to A. Z.'s concluding words. As for Frank, he was evidently in quite a deep state of perplexity and doubt.

"A. Z.," he exclaimed, "I never heard of a great painter called Bondoné !"

"Very likely not, Frank," answered A. Z., coolly. "I don't think I ever did either."

"Then how *can* you tell such a—!" Tom was beginning, in virtuous indignation, when A. Z. laughed, and took the words out of his mouth.

"How can I tell such a story? Well, Tom, I tell it because the story is true. I say I have never heard of a painter called Bondoné—nor have I—but remember my shepherd-boy had another name that you have never heard yet. His full name was Ambrogiotto Bondoné; and we shorten that, and call him simply—GIOTTO."

"Oh! and is that really Giotto's story?" said Frank with the clear eyes.

"I never heard of *him* any more than the other," said Tom, returning to his noughts and crosses.

"The more shame to you, Tom," answered A. Z.

The next day was Sunday, and, as a certain amount of quietness had always been required from the children on that day, A. Z. would probably have found it tolerably easy to get through the portion of it during which they were at home without any story-telling : however, as it turned out, in the course of the evening, as they sat round the fire, rather by chance than anything else, a little story did get told to them. They were not all present at it. Dick and Tom had gone away after afternoon church for a long ramble, and had not yet returned, and Peggy was learning hymns seated at the farthest window. A. Z. had drawn her chair before the fire, and Kitty and Frank and Gracie were the three who were beside her.

"We shall soon have fires again all day long," said Frank, sitting on the hearthrug and looking meditatively before him. "Do you like that time, A. Z.?"

"Yes, Frank," answered A. Z., "but I like summer better."

"*I* don't," said Kitty, with decision. "I like fires indoors, and ice, and snow, and frost."

"Frost and snow are very pretty," said Frank; "but not so pretty as flowers. I like the time best when the flowers first begin."

"Do you, Frankie?" asked A. Z., and she put her hand softly on Frank's head. "Then you and I agree together, for I was taught long ago to love spring best."

"Who taught you, A. Z.?" asked Kitty, who seldom had any scruples about asking anything.

A. Z. said nothing for a moment or two; but then she told them.

STORY THE THIRD.

LITTLE JOHNNY.

A LITTLE boy taught me, Kitty [said A. Z.];
a child I lived with once long ago. I was
a little girl then, but he was younger than
I was, and when we played together I used
to take care of him. For there was a sad
thing about him. Once, when he was very
little indeed, some one who had the care of
him had let him fall, and he was lame and could
not walk. I don't mean only a little lame, but so
helpless that we used to carry him about in our
arms; I was only four years older than he was, but
he was such a little weakly thing that when he was
five or six I could hold him in my arms for an hour
at a time. It was a very sad thing. The person
who let him fall—never mind who it was—almost
broke her heart when she knew what she had done.

G

We were all very fond of him. Nobody could have helped being that, for you can't think how gentle and good he was. He suffered so much, and yet none of the rest of us, who were well from morning to night, ever were so gentle and good as he. Many people who have a great deal of illness to bear become selfish, and behave as if they thought the world ought to be turned upside down to find relief for them ; but our little Johnny never seemed to think that he was worth one-half of the care that we bestowed upon him. It was almost painful to see how grateful he was to everybody who was kind to him.

He was very fond of me [said A. Z., in a low voice]. There were a good many more of us in the house, but out of us all he and I clung together most. I don't know whether *I* loved *him* more than the rest did—we were all so fond of him ; but perhaps I did. Many a day, for hours together, we two would be alone. There was a window high up in the house, where few people came ; it was only a staircase window, but it looked out over miles of gardens, and green fields, and trees, and we would sit there at it for hours on the stairs together. Sometimes he would sit beside me, but oftener I held him in my arms. He used to lie with his head on my shoulder, and his face turned to the fields, and there for hours we would talk together, or he would tell me stories [better stories than these I tell to you, children, said A. Z. with a smile], the wildest, sweetest stories that I think it ever entered into a child's head to conceive. He was a little fellow, not so old as you, Frankie, when he used to pour them out to me, and in all the years I have lived since I have never heard the like of them again. They were like golden dreams of some other world. Sometimes, when he would tell them to me on summer evenings, lying in the fields perhaps, or by the sea shore, with his face to the sunset, I almost used to think he was reading them, in some way that no one else could read, out of the wild colours in the sky.

He was four years younger than I, but when I was ten years old and he was six, he would talk to me of things that I had never thought of—grave, solemn things that he himself had never been told of—that no one had ever spoken to him about. They came into his head, he said.

They were always coming into his head; he never lay for ten minutes without speaking in my arms but at the end of them he was full of some new thought. I can hear his little voice yet as it used to break the silence so many many times with its soft, "Sister, I wonder—"

I was very proud of him—I thought there was no one like him in the world. I got so used to seeing him weak and ill that his puniness and help-lessness did not seem the same to me that they did to other people. *I* only saw how clever and good he was, and many a time I used to talk to him of how he would be a great man when he grew up. I never doubted that he would; I was so proud of everything he did and said. All his strange thoughts and questions, and his wild sweet stories, seemed such wonderful things to me.

We were always together, and we thought we could not live without each other. He often put his arms about my neck, and said to me, "You must never go away from me, Sister;" and the thought that he wanted me, and would always want me, used, I remember, to make me happier than almost anything in the world.

With all his thoughtfulness and his grave earnest ways, he was so childlike, too,—so easily pleased, so easily grieved, so religious, so pure-hearted. Never was there any one more easily amused than he was. He would sit and play for hours at the most childish game, quite content if only some one that he loved was at his side.

To care for spring was one of the many things he taught me,—for he was always teaching me

something; he taught me the beginnings of most
of the things I know now. He himself loved spring-
time as I never have known it loved by any other
child. We always in the house used to speak as if
the spring of the year in a sort belonged to him; and
so it did. It was *his* time; he was born in spring
[A. Z. paused for a moment, and then said very
softly]; and it was in spring that he died.

All the years that I had been with him I never
had known or guessed that it was likely he would
die. All the elder people in the house had long
known it, but it never was told to me. I only
knew it at the close of the last year before the
spring in which we lost him.

From the beginning of that winter he was very
weak, so much so that after the end of autumn he
never went out. The autumn had been a very beautiful one, and I remember very well that almost to
the end of October there were days so warm that
we had been able to sit out in the open air for hours
together. The last day that year on which he sat
out so was the last day on which he ever went into
the fields. It was a mild, bright day, and we sat
together at the foot of a haystack till the sun had
almost set. He was very well that day, and, leaning on me with my arm about him, he had been
telling me a long story. It was so long that a good

while before it was ended I said we must go home, and we settled that we would come again to-morrow to the same place and have it finished. But in the night the weather changed. We woke up next morning to find that winter had come; there was thick hoar frost on the ground, and a great wind sweeping the trees bare. I never before or since saw a winter settle down upon us with such a sudden grasp as that one. Our garden had been full of flowers only yesterday, and to-day there was not one that was not broken and withered by the frost. By a week's end all the country was lying under snow.

The last glimpse he ever had of summer was that hour when he sat with me under the haystack; he never lived to see another summer come back. During the whole winter he scarcely left the house. It was bitterly cold—the longest and most unbroken cold I ever felt. You would have liked it, Kitty, for there was ice, and snow, and frost in abundance, and sharp winds too, and we had to burn such fires in the house as we had never burnt before. But our poor little lad did not like it. He longed to go out into the fresh air again, and, except three or four times during five months, we never dared to take him out; and he pined and wasted so in the house. If we could have taken him to a warmer climate it probably would have done him good, but after the winter had once set in—and I told you how suddenly it came—it was so cold that the doctor who saw him would not let him be moved.

Children [said A. Z.], it was the saddest winter I ever spent, and yet there was that in it, even through all its sadness, that made it dearer to all of us than almost any year of our lives. No other year has ever been so dear to *me*.

For a long time, I told you, I did not know that he was dying. I saw that he was more delicate than usual, and weaker, but he did not suffer more pain than at other times, and his weakness, I thought, only came from his being kept so long indoors. I never doubted that he would be better when the spring came.

The winter had begun before the end of October, and it was not until the last day of the old year that I knew for the first time that it was likely he would not live.

He had been very unwell that day, and we had taken him early to bed, but he could not sleep, and after some time I came and lay down upon the bed beside him, and put his head upon my shoulder, for often when he was restless he used to like to lie so, and to have me sing to him. So I began to sing very softly, and though it did not make him sleep he soon lay quite content and still, looking up into my face.

After a little while, once when I had stopped singing, he said softly—

" I wonder if the old year minds dying, Sister."

I smiled and said I did not know, and then for a few minutes I lay without speaking, thinking of many things that had happened during the long year that was ending.

I had not spoken again when he said—

" If I fall asleep would you wake me ?—because I want to see the old year die."

It had always been a fancy with him to see the old years dying, but to-night he was ill, and I knew our mother would not like him to be awake so late, so I said—

" Not to-night, Johnny. Never mind it for once."

But he crept nearer to me, and put his arm about my neck, and said wistfully—

" It is for the last time, Sister."

I called out sharply—"Johnny !"

For an instant I tried to think that he was dreaming, and I pressed my arm closer round him, and said—"What do you mean, dear ?"

Then he looked into my face, and said—

" I shall never see another old year die, Sister ; because, before the next year goes away, *I* shall be dead."

Children [said A. Z., in a very low voice], many years have passed away since then, but I think something broke in my heart that night that has never got mended since.

I believed what he told me, and I did right to believe, for it was as he said. But how he himself had guessed it we never knew; we could only tell that he had found it out for himself in the strange quiet way in which he had always learnt so many things. I used often to think that he could read other people's thoughts, and could see in our mother's face when she bent over him all that there was about him in her heart.

That night, when the old year passed away, I felt as if I had shut the door upon all my life that had gone before. From that night everything was new and different. I rose up on the first morning of the new year as if it were to a new world. My little lad and I had grown together, side by side, in a sort of double life, and now for the first time I knew that I must learn to live alone.

I will not make you sad by telling you much about the months that followed. I know how sorry you would have been for him if you could have seen him as he was wasting away—but all his suffering is over long, long ago, and my darling is a thousand times happier now than we who sit talking of him here.

It was on the last day of the year that he told me he was dying, and God gave him to us for four months more. I told you what a long cold winter it was; the snow came early, and stayed late, so that again and again to the very middle of April we used to rise in the mornings and find the hills white. I think we never wearied and longed so for spring in all our lives as we did then. We wanted it so for *him*, because it was the one thing that he seemed to yearn to see before he died—looking for it day and night with his wistful eyes. He longed for it so, that when, one day before March was gone, I found two or three primroses in the fields and brought them home to him, he couldn't speak to me when I gave them to him, but at the first sight of them burst into tears. My little lad!—he has seen sweeter flowers than those since.

He longed for spring, and he saw it before he left us. For one fortnight—that was all. It was the last half of April; on the first of May—May-day—as bright and beautiful a May-day as ever dawned, he died.

I remember that last fortnight as, even now, the most sacred time I have ever spent; we knew during the whole of it that the end might come any day, almost any hour, but there was no loud sorrow on account of it in any of us; it seemed as if we all were able during those days to put away our tears.

He used to lie on his little couch in the sunshine, faded and wasted to a shadow, but with his face as clear and bright as the sunlight was itself. He had no pain at that time at all—whatever he had suffered was past—he was simply sinking into his rest. Falling into it, too, without any, even the slightest, shadow of fear. The two worlds scarcely seemed to him, I think, *like* two ; heaven had always been so near to him that I think there was scarcely any feeling in him now of a journey to be taken. It was only a quiet happy sense of going "home." Going to God and Christ—to the Father who had made him, and the Lord who loved him.

He died, I told you, upon May-day. It was in the afternoon, when the bright day was at its fullest. I had been all the morning with him. He had only been able to speak a very little, but he had asked me to read to him, and I had been reading, and two or three times when I had put the Bible away, he had asked me to go on again, and I had done so.

In the afternoon, when we were all with him, I read to him for the last time. I read until I came to these words :—

"*Suffer little children to come unto me, and forbid them not, for of such is the kingdom of God.*"

And then I could not read any more. I went on my knees at his bedside, and hid my face over his hands.

I remember now as if it was yesterday the long solemn silence that there was as I knelt there—and then the sound that broke it. It was a faint sound that came suddenly—a low cry—and there was a stir, and as I raised my head I saw his face.

I knew then what was coming—we all knew, and we closed round him, and kissed him. Our little one! There was neither sorrow nor pain in his face then. *I* kissed him last, and the last word my darling said in this world was my name.

———•••———

A. Z.'s voice trembled as she left off speaking. The children had hitherto been ready enough with questions and remarks at the close of a story, but the three who had listened to this one said nothing when it ended; only after a minute little Gracie came close to A. Z.'s side, and reached up her arm about her neck.

Then A. Z. smiled, and took Gracie on her knee and kissed her; but neither of them spoke, and Gracie said afterwards that A. Z.'s cheek as it touched her's was quite wet.

"Do tell us a pretty story to-day, A. Z.," said Kitty, quite piteously, next afternoon.

"I shall be very glad, Kitty," answered A. Z. "What shall I tell you?"

"Oh, something nice: not like Saturday's one," said Kitty bluntly.

"So you didn't like Saturday's story, Kitty?" inquired A. Z. laughing.

"I didn't like it *much*," said Kitty prudently.

"You didn't like it a *bit*, Kitty—you know you didn't!" cried plain-spoken Tom.

"Well, Tom, you know you can't expect Kitty's tastes yet to be as ripe and sound as yours," said A. Z. gravely. "What pleased you so much would naturally perhaps be a little beyond her."

"Oh, A. Z.!" shouted Tom; and he was so much amused at the notion that *he* had especially enjoyed Saturday's story that he quite went off into a roar.

"But, A. Z., he *didn't* like it; neither Tom nor Dick listened to half of it!" eagerly explained Peggy, who always took everything just as it was said.

"Did they really not? Why didn't you tell me that before, Peggy?" gravely inquired A. Z.

"But we *did* listen to a great deal of it," said Dick apologetically, feeling a little uneasy in his mind, and not quite sure if A. Z. was serious in her surprise or not.

"No doubt, Dick," replied A. Z. "Some people, I've heard, always have their minds more freely at their disposal when they have first set their fingers to work. I daresay it's so with you and Tom. Did you ever try noughts and crosses over a hard bit of Latin or Greek?"

"Oh, you're quizzing us, A. Z!" cried Dick, beginning to laugh.

"But about to-day's story, A. Z.?" said Kitty, returning with decision to the matter in hand.

"Well, Kitty, with respect to to-day's story, I must see what I can do," said A. Z.

"Tell us a jolly story, A. Z.," said Tom.

"Oh yes, a funny story!" cried little Gracie.

"I'll do the best I can, Gracie," answered A. Z. "So go to your seats."

They went to their seats accordingly, and A. Z. began.

STORY THE FOURTH.

ADVENTURES OF SO-FAT AND MEW-MEW.

PART THE FIRST.

"GET out of the way!" said a little black dog, pushing up to the warmest place before the kitchen fire.

"Get out of the way yourself!" answered a little white puss, who had got the best place there before him.

"You're the most spoiled, vicious, selfish little beast I ever came across!" cried the little dog, whose name was So-Fat, in a rage.

"I'm not half so spoiled nor so selfish as you!" snapped out the little cat, who was called Mew-Mew.

["Oh, A. Z.!" cried Gracie, clapping her hands, having with difficulty restrained herself so far. For

Gracie thought there was nothing in the world half so delightful to talk about as little cats and dogs.

"Hold your tongue, Grace!" cried Tom, with dignified severity, thinking within himself that both Gracie and A. Z. were trifling in a most childish way.

Then A. Z. went on.]

So-Fat and Mew-Mew were a very young dog and cat, and their education had been a good deal neglected, or else, no doubt, they would never have allowed themselves to use such language as this to one another. But they were a poor little pair of orphans, or as good as orphans, for they had quite lost sight of their fathers and mothers, and never had been taught polite behaviour by anybody. They had not indeed the least idea of such a thing, and, so far from shewing courtesy and respect to one another, they were each continually exclaiming that they could not see for what purpose on earth the other *could* have been born.

"Such a useless, lazy, vain, ill-tempered, cowardly creature!" So-Fat would say.

"Such a pert, noisy, selfish, greedy, irritating thing!" Mew-Mew would answer.

"Of all creatures in the world, a cat is certainly the most utterly useless!" So-Fat would exclaim.

" Of all worries in a house, there's nothing like a dog!" would scream Mew-Mew.

And in this way they used to go on half the day. It was quite a mercy whenever they fell asleep, for that was about the only time when their tongues were quiet.

Besides this trouble that each had with the other, you must also know that both So-Fat and Mew-Mew were exceedingly discontented with the world in general. They had faults to find with everything. They did not like the house they lived in, and they did not like the people they lived with, and they thought they never got enough either to eat or to drink, and So-Fat was always grumbling because there were no other little dogs like himself about the place, so that he could never, he said, get a good game of play; and Mew-Mew would sit with her eyes half shut for hours, thinking what a cruel thing it was that she had not a bit of company from one week's end to another.

" Now, if *I* had a house," Mew-Mew would say to herself, " I'd have at least a dozen kittens in it, and I'd have fires in all the rooms, winter and summer, and warm milk always standing on the floors, and the larder-door should always be open, with all the meat inside cut up into small pieces. And I'd put to death every dog in the world ! "

H

And then the picture of the life she would lead would get so delightful to Mew-Mew that she would burst out purring, and never leave off till she had sung herself to sleep.

"Did ever any one see such a fool!" So-Fat would exclaim, coming in sometimes and seeing her. "Singing to herself as if she was out of her wits! Well, I've seen many things in my life" (So-Fat was full six months old, so of course he had), "I've seen many things, but I never saw anything yet so absurd as that!"

And then very likely he would go up to her, and out of pure contempt would give her a blow on the side of her head—upon which, of course, Mew-Mew would spring up like a shot, and, unless So-Fat took to his heels with all his might (and he generally did take to his heels pretty quickly when Mew-Mew's wrath was up), there would be a pitched battle between them on the spot.

So-Fat and Mew-Mew lived in a farm house, and you will be sorry to hear how perpetually the poor ill-used things were being irritated by one animal or another. There were first the chickens. Mew-Mew could not bear the chickens. "Such impudent, audacious things! Eating, too, from morning to night," Mew-Mew used to say contemptuously,— though Mew-Mew would dearly have liked to have been doing the same herself. Then the pigs. So-Fat hated the pigs. " They're the ugliest, dirtiest, stupidest beasts on the whole farm," cried So-Fat ; who one day, in a great fit of courage, had walked into the pig-sty to bark at the pigs, and had, nearly got trodden to death for his pains ; such absurd creatures as the pigs were. Then the ducks. If there was one thing Mew-Mew hated more than another, it was the ill-bred, noisy way the ducks went on. And so it was with everything. It was quite clear that there never before had been a little cat and dog so unkindly treated and persecuted as So-Fat and Mew-Mew. They had not a single thing that they wanted, and nothing but worry and trouble on every hand ; and as for their masters and mistresses, if *they* did not exactly do all they could to torment them, at least they did not prevent the chickens and the pigs, and the ducks and geese, and cows and horses, and everything else upon the farm from doing so ; and at any rate it *was* certainly their fault that So-Fat had no companions like himself, and that Mew-Mew had not got her fellow-kittens, and that the fires were not always a-light, and the warm milk on the floors, and the larder door open : there was no doubt of that.

So, Gracie [said A. Z.], I hope you are very sorry indeed for poor little unkindly-treated So-Fat and Mew-Mew.

[Gracie looked rather grave at this appeal. Well, yes, certainly, she *was* sorry ; but, on the whole, she did not feel altogether sure that the case was quite so dreadful a one as A. Z. seemed to say it was. She remembered last winter how a little kitten had come one dark, cold night crying to the house door—a homeless little cat, without a bit of flesh that could be felt between its poor coat and its little bones; the sight of it was very nearly breaking little Gracie's heart, and she could not but think that matters were a long way off being so bad as that with either So-Fat or Mew-Mew. But still she did look grave. It was no doubt a sad case, too.]

When So-Fat and Mew-Mew were both about nine months old [A. Z. went on], it happened that one day So-Fat got into trouble. He had gone into the barnyard for no harm at all except to bark at the chickens, and put them all in a fright. In particular, he was getting some rare fun out of one foolish little chicken, who had got into such a state of alarm that she had run away to her roost, and perched herself on the top of it, while So-Fat down on the ground was barking with all his might, and making springs up at her into the air, and really was, just for once, almost as happy as he could desire, when the saddest thing happened—one of the jumps he made brought down a great beam of wood upon him, and in a moment poor little So-Fat was howling so that you might have heard him half a mile away.   Half a dozen people came running at the noise as hard as they could pelt, and when they raised up the great piece of wood, besides a number of hard bruises, one of So-Fat's little front legs was found broken right across.   So a doctor had to be sent for, and the leg to be dressed, and then So-Fat had to be put to bed.

As soon as ever he was in bed, and his masters and mistresses, who had all gathered round him, were gone out of the kitchen again, up came Mew-Mew to him, arching her back, and mincing her steps, and looking as wicked and conceited as you please.

"Well, you've come to a pretty pass now!" said Mew-Mew, looking at him.

"Oh—h—h!" groaned So-Fat; for the poor little beast was in a great deal of pain.

"It's nothing but what you deserve.   I only wonder you did'nt break *all* your legs.   It'll be a pretty time before *you* get about again!" said Mew-Mew.

"You hold your tongue—you'd better!" growled So-Fat in a terrible rage, and he gave her a look as if he could have skinned and eaten her on the spot.

"You hold your own tongue, or I'll make it the worse for you!" answered Mew-Mew, and up she put her paw, and gave So-Fat a push that made the poor little dog howl out with pain.

Upon that, all the masters and mistresses came running into the room again to see what ever the matter could be, and Mew-Mew, who, to tell the truth, was rather frightened at what she had done, slunk out of the kitchen between their feet. She took care to keep out of everybody's way for the rest of that day, and it was only when it was pretty late, and every body had gone to bed, that she ventured to steal into the kitchen again, and take up her place before the fire.

So-Fat was in his little bed, with the clothes tucked round him.

[" Oh, A. Z.," cried Gracie, breaking in in great excitement, " did they really give him bed-clothes ?"

"Yes, Gracie—a feather bed, and bolster, and pillow, and sheets, and blankets," answered A. Z.]

Well, he was lying in his little bed with the clothes tucked round him, but he wasn't asleep, for he was in so much pain that he couldn't go to sleep at all, and when he saw Mew-Mew steal in through a hole that was made in the kitchen door on purpose for her, he got in such a fright, that he didn't know what to do, for after the way in which she had behaved to him in the afternoon, he didn't feel at all sure but what now, when every body was in bed, she might kill him outright. It was a terrible situation for So-Fat. He shut his eyes, all but the least bit, just enough for him to look out through and see what Mew-Mew was doing, and then he lay as still as a mouse, except that, to be sure, he was trembling in every limb.

Mew-Mew walked in, and gave a side glance to So-Fat's bed, and then, seeing him, as she thought, fast asleep, she cautiously came forward to the fire, and, sitting down there with her back to him (which she thought was the best way to prevent him seeing her), she began to wash her coat, and was soon so deeply interested in that occupation, that she quite, for the time, forgot all about So-Fat, and everything else.   For Mew-Mew had a beautiful milk white coat, upon which it was her custom to spend hours and hours every day—washing so hard at it that So-Fat had many a time said sneeringly, he wondered it wasn't washed away; but Mew-Mew never minded that a bit, for she knew that it was only said out of envy.   For So-Fat himself was as black as a coal.

So Mew-Mew sat washing herself, and So-Fat lay trembling and looking at her, afraid to shut his eyes completely and try to go to sleep, for fear of the consequences, till he was perfectly tired and worn out, and was in such a rage with Mew-Mew for giving herself such a prodigious wash, that he scarcely knew what to do.   His poor little leg was aching so, too, that at last, after Mew-Mew had washed herself for an hour and a half without stopping, he couldn't stand it any longer, but, not caring what came of it, he turned himself in his bed, and gave a great groan. At which Mew-Mew stopped lathering herself in an instant.

"I'll groan again," thought So-Fat. "I may as well as I've done it once." So he groaned again accordingly, and over and over again after that, for he found it a great relief, and, if he *was* to be killed, he felt of course that he had better try to get as much satisfaction as he could out of existing circumstances, as long as he had the power.

When she heard him groaning so very loud, Mew-Mew, you may be sure, was not long in turning round.

"Oh, you're awake, are you?" said Mew-Mew.

"Oh—h—h yes, I'm awake," answered So-Fat.

And then there came another groan, almost as if he was at his last breath.

"Do you mean to go on making that noise all night?" cried Mew-Mew, looking very fierce.

"*I* don't know," answered So-Fat, quite recklessly; and he made a plunge in his bed that quite upset the blankets.

"Well, *you're* a grateful beast!" said Mew-Mew, looking sternly at him. "There you lie on a feather-bed, with blankets and sheets, and I don't know

what all, while all *I've* got in the world to lie on is
an old bit of rug, and yet you must go on groaning
as if you were being killed. It would better become
me to groan," said Mew-Mew.

"You! A pretty story! I wish you had my
leg!" cried poor So-Fat.

"Oh, we shall never hear the last of that leg
now," said Mew-Mew, shrugging her shoulders; and,
as she had nothing more to say, she curled herself
up on her rug, and went off to sleep.

But she had only slept for a very little while,
and had just fallen into a most delicious dream
about a mouse, when she was awakened by a doleful cry from So-Fat.

"Mew-Mew!" cried So-Fat.

"What's the matter now?" demanded Mew-Mew,
lifting up her head in a great rage.

"Oh, I'm dying with thirst! Do fetch me a
drop of water," cried So-Fat.

"Well, it will be a pretty thing if *I'm* to be kept
awake all night to nurse you," said Mew-Mew very
sulkily; but, however, she got up, and pushed So-
Fat's bowl of water up to his side, and held it between her paws for him while he drank.

"Oh, I feel better now," said So-Fat, when he had
quite emptied the bowl. "If it wasn't for the pain
in my leg, I really think, Mew-Mew, that I could go
to sleep."

"I wish you would, and let other people go to sleep too," answered Mew-Mew severely; and with that she marched back to the fire and curled herself up on the rug, and went soundly off again.

But she had hardly slept for half-an-hour when So-Fat was shouting to her once more.

"Mew-Mew! Oh, *Mew-Mew!*"

"What on earth is it now?" cried Mew-Mew, getting up angrier than ever.

"I'm so hot I think I shall die!" said So-Fat.

"I wish you *were* dead," answered Mew-Mew. "What's the use of awaking me to tell me that?"

"Oh, but I want you to pull away these clothes from me," cried So-Fat.

"Oh, dear, dear!" said Mew-Mew. But she went and pulled away the clothes, and took care to throw a good warm blanket over towards the fire, so that she might have a comfortable sleep upon it presently.

"Well, are you content now?" said Mew-Mew, when she had taken everything away from him.

"Oh, I don't know; I'm very ill," said So-Fat; and he puffed and panted, and gave the most doleful look into Mew-Mew's face.

"I daresay you're not a bit worse than I am myself," answered Mew-Mew; "you've got nothing like such a cold as I have on my chest."

"A cold on your chest!" echoed So-Fat. "What's a cold on your chest compared with a broken leg!"

"Oh, there you are — beginning about your leg again!" cried Mew-Mew; and off she went straight to the fire, and settled herself for another sleep.

She slept this time for a good long while, and So-Fat slept too, but just as it was coming towards day-break, a louder cry than ever rose up in the room.

"Oh, Mew-Mew! *Mew-Mew!* Mew-Mew!" cried So-Fat.

"Dear me! dear me! what *is* it now?" said Mew-Mew.

"I can't bear it any longer! You must come and loosen this bandage," cried So-Fat.

"Any thing for peace," said Mew-Mew; and up she came and bit the fastenings of the bandage, and took it off.

"Well, are you right now?" asked Mew-Mew.

"I'm better," said So-Fat. But he lay back on his pillow quite exhausted.

"You don't look to me as if you'd live," said Mew-Mew, after she had stood and looked at him for some moments.

"Not look as if I should live!" echoed So-Fat, quite confounded, for he had never thought of anything half so dreadful.

"No, *I* don't think you do," answered Mew-Mew; and with that she sat down before him with her eyes fixed on his face, as if she meant to wait there and see the end of him.

"Oh, dear, dear!" cried So-Fat; and the perspiration began to stand out on his forehead, he was in such a fright.

"Is there—is there anything you think I could do, Mew-Mew?" he asked presently in a feeble voice.

"Oh, *I* don't know of anything," answered Mew-Mew. "You must just wait." And she shut her eyes softly, as if she thought there might possibly be time before she was wanted at the end for a little doze.

"But, Mew-Mew, Mew-Mew!" cried poor So-Fat, "you mustn't go to sleep! Oh, Mew-Mew, I've got nobody to speak to but you!"

"Speaking won't help you," answered Mew-Mew; "you were always too fond of speaking. I've told you that myself, So-Fat, over and over again."

"Yes, Mew-Mew, so you have," said So-Fat, quite humbly. "But you surely would not have me d-die without saying anything, would you? I've so *many* things I should like to say! Oh, Mew-Mew, what will you do without me when I'm g-g-gone?"

The poor little dog gave such a doleful look into

Mew-Mew's face as he spoke these words that Mew-Mew did not quite know what to say.   To tell the truth, though she tried to think that she was very glad at this near prospect of getting rid of So-Fat for good and all, yet she was not altogether comfortable about it.   After all, it would be an odd world without So-Fat.   However, she did not like to shew that she was so changeable and weak as to feel that, so when So Fat said—"What will you do when I'm gone?" she answered pretty coolly—

"Oh, I'll do just as usual, I suppose."

And then she pretended to see a speck on one of her white paws, and began furiously to wash it off.

But poor little So-Fat was in such a state of distress that he could not bear this.

"What—you'll do just as usual—without *me*?" cried So-Fat.   "You'll go on just the same when you'll never have me to look at—or to speak to—or to-to f-fight with?"   And at that last tender inquiry So-Fat's voice quite broke down.   "Oh, Mew-Mew, you heartless creature!"

"I'm *not* a heartless creature!" cried Mew-Mew, and she almost began to sob.   "If it comes to that, you're ten times more heartless than I am."

"*Me* heartless!" cried So-Fat.

"Yes, you are!   You don't care for me," cried Mew-Mew, "a bit more than if I was a chicken or a pig.   You would not sit up with me as I'm sitting with you now—not if I'd broken all the legs I've got."

"Oh, Mew-Mew, how can you say such things?" cried So-Fat.   "Oh, Mew-Mew, how *can* you—and me dying?"

"You would not care if *I* was dying fifty times over," said Mew-Mew.   And she put her paw over her face and began to cry.

"I-I-I *would!*" sobbed So-Fat.   "I'm sure I've always liked you—but it's you that never were willing to make friends.   You never cou-cou-could bear me," said So-Fat.

"*Me* never bear you!   Well! well!" cried Mew-Mew.

And then she sat and rocked herself to and fro, and—would you believe it?—she thought she was the most misunderstood cat, and So-Fat thought he was the most misunderstood dog that ever had lived.

"I'm sure I don't want not to be friends with you, now you're going out of the world," said Mew-Mew presently, looking up, and wiping her eyes.

"Well, let us shake hands," said So-Fat in a broken voice.

So he put out one of his fore-paws, and Mew-Mew, very much affected, took and pressed it between both of hers.   Then they were both quite quiet for several minutes, for they were so much moved by what had taken place that neither of them was able to speak.

Mew-Mew was the first after some time to break the silence.

"How *do* you feel yourself now, So-Fat?" she said.

"Not quite so faint," answered So-Fat. "If you *could* get me a little more water, dear Mew-Mew."

"With pleasure!" cried Mew-Mew. And she hurried away, and got the water, and held it to So-Fat's lips.

"How do I look now, Mew-Mew?" asked So-Fat, when he had laid his head back on the pillow, and he gave the most piteous look you can imagine into Mew-Mew's face.

"Ah, not very well!" said Mew-Mew, sorrowfully. "There's a look in your eyes I don't like."

"Oh! if it's only my eyes," said So-Fat, hopefully, "I could alter that. Look at me now, Mew-Mew."

And he changed his doleful look for one so bright and sharp that Mew-Mew clapped her paws with delight, and cried out—"Oh, that's quite another thing! Why, your eyes are as bright as mine now, So-Fat!"

"No, no—not so bright as *yours*," said So-Fat gallantly. "No other eyes could be as bright as yours,

Mew-Mew. But I *do* feel better, and I can't help thinking, dear Mew-Mew, that if I could get a re-freshing sleep, and a little nourishing food "——

"Should you like a mouse?" cried Mew-Mew with eagerness.

"Ah—it would be too exciting, I'm afraid," said So-Fat sadly. "No—I must not take stimulants, Mew-Mew—they might bring on fever. But per-haps the boiled wing of a chicken, or a little cold mutton—under-done."

"Well—I'll try what I can do," said Mew-Mew.

So away she went, and prowled in all directions, but the only thing she could find (for the larder was locked as usual) was a plate of sandwiches on a shelf. However, sandwiches were not bad food, Mew-Mew remembered; so, after tasting two or three to see that they were well made, she went back to So-Fat with her prize.

"What is it, Mew-Mew?" asked So-Fat eagerly.

"Sandwiches," answered Mew-Mew. "Delicious ones!" And she held the plate up to him.

"Keep me company, dear Mew-Mew," said So-Fat, helping himself to the largest one in the dish.

"Well, I don't care if I do," said Mew-Mew. "The morning air gives one an appetite." And she fell to work without the loss of another moment.

In a very few minutes the plate was quite empty.

"It has been very pleasant!" said So-Fat, lean ing back with a sigh.

"*Very* pleasant!" answered Mew-Mew, licking the plate to catch the last crumbs.

"It has done me a great deal of good. There's no more of it, I suppose?" said So-Fat, wistfully.

"Not another morsel!" answered Mew-Mew.

"Well, it can't be helped," said So-Fat, resignedly. "Shall I try now to go to sleep?"

"Do," answered Mew-Mew; "and I'll shake up your pillows for you."

So she did that, and arranged the clothes neatly, and then So-Fat lay down and shut his eyes.

"I'll just give myself a slight wash, and then follow your example," said Mew-Mew. "Be sure you call me if you feel worse, dear So-Fat."

"Oh, yes, I'll call you," answered So-Fat, half asleep already.

So Mew-Mew washed herself carefully all over, and then, seeing So-Fat quite quiet and comfortable, she rolled herself up on one of his blankets, and slept soundly till the servants came down stairs and opened the shutters.

I dare say you won't be much surprised to hear that, in spite of this fright which they had had, So-Fat wasn't in the least danger of dying at all.

Nobody ever thought of such a thing except himself and Mew-Mew. So, though he occasionally brought on a good deal of fever by over-eating himself, and though he had to stay in bed for a whole week, and for a week or ten days more was rather weak, and obliged to be careful of himself, yet by the end of a month he was as strong again as ever, and quite as ready to bark at the pigs, and worry the chickens, as he had ever been. "Don't run into danger—*don't*, So-Fat! For *my* sake!" Mew-Mew would say to him a dozen times a day—but it wasn't a bit of use; he was running into danger and into mischief all day long.

He and Mew-Mew were the closest and dearest friends now. Mew-Mew always thought and said that it was her good nursing that had saved his life, and So-Fat, from hearing Mew-Mew declare it so often, got quite to believe this too, and he thought that Mew-Mew was the best friend he had in the world. As for Mew-Mew, she became so fond of So-Fat, that she could scarcely bear to have him out of her sight ; and in fact, they loved each other now so much, that in course of time they both came quite to forget that they had ever hated one another, and wouldn't have believed it if you had told them.

But, though they were so delighted with each other, they weren't a bit more pleased than they had been with the rest of the world; indeed, they soon came to think a good deal worse of the universe than ever, for, whereas before they had had nobody to speak to about their wrongs and troubles, they could now talk together about all these things—and everybody knows how very big a grievance may be made by talking of it, when both the talkers take the same side.   In fact, by talking, the world before long became so very black, and dismal, and hopeless, in the sight of So-Fat and Mew-Mew, that the only wonder was how they possibly managed to go on living in it at all.

At last matters came to a head.

One night, after all the house had gone to bed, and So-Fat and Mew-Mew met together, as they always did now at that time, to have a quiet talk before the kitchen fire, So-Fat began the conversa tion with these terrible words :—

"I wish everybody was dead!" said So-Fat.

"Oh, So-Fat!   But not *me*?" cried Mew-Mew, all in a flutter.

"No—not you.   But everybody else," answered So-Fat, in deep despair.

"Dear! dear!   What is it in particular?" inquired Mew-Mew.

"It's the pigs," answered So-Fat, gloomily.

"What have they been doing?" asked Mew-Mew, anxiously.

"Grunting," answered So-Fat, with indignation.

"But they haven't been touching you, have they?" said Mew-Mew.

"They would have touched me if they could," replied So-Fat.

And then there was a long pause. Mew-Mew was the first to renew the conversation.

"Well, pigs *are* a disgrace to a place," said Mew-Mew, sympathetically; "but yet, do you know, So-Fat, all things considered, I'm not so sure but chickens are worse."

"Chickens are bad enough," returned So-Fat; "they're vicious things. But for real spite, there's nothing like pigs."

"Perhaps you're right," said Mew-Mew, thoughtfully. "Yet I don't know but what, out of the whole set, I could believe worst of all of ducks."

"There's scarcely a shade to choose between them," said So-Fat. "That's the truth."

And then he began to groan. And as soon as he gave one groan, Mew-Mew gave another, and so they kept it up for five minutes.

"I've a good mind not to bear it," said So-Fat at last.

"Dear me, how can you help bearing it, So-Fat?" cried Mew-Mew, opening her eyes.

"I could go away," said So-Fat.

" Where to ?" screamed Mew-Mew.

" Anywhere !" said So-Fat, solemnly.

But Mew-Mew was so overwhelmed by this announcement, that for a few moments she couldn't utter a word.   At last, when she had recovered her voice again—

" Oh, So-Fat, you wouldn't leave *me*, would you ?" she said.

" Wouldn't you come with me, Mew-Mew ?" asked So-Fat.   And he put on such a tender look, that Mew-Mew was quite overpowered.

" Anywhere !—to the end of the world !" answered Mew-Mew, putting up her paw to hide her tears.

" Then we will go together," said So-Fat solemnly. And then they didn't speak another word for five minutes, they were so much moved.

" It must be a change for the better, wherever we go ; that's clear at any rate," said So-Fat, breaking the silence first.

" Yes ; that's *quite* clear," answered Mew-Mew.

" And perhaps they'll learn to value us here, when—when we're gone," said So-Fat, quite affected.

" When it's too late," said Mew-Mew.

" Yes, when it's too late," echoed So-Fat, with a deep sigh.

And then Mew-Mew sighed, and then they both sighed together.

" When shall we set off?" said Mew-Mew.

" Now!—this moment!" answered So-Fat, start-ing up, and waving his paw.

" But all the doors are locked!" cried Mew-Mew, in a great flutter.   (For, to tell the truth, Mew-Mew did not feel quite so eager about this expedition as So-Fat did, she being by nature a great stay-at-home, and, with regard to this night in particular, she had been laying her account for hours past with having a comfortable sleep, and really she didn't feel in a fit state either of mind or body to assent to So-Fat's proposal. So—) " All the doors are locked!" cried Mew-Mew.   " And, besides, I'm not washed!"

" Can't you live a single night without being washed?" cried So-Fat, getting into a rage.

" Live without being washed!   I should think not!" exclaimed Mew-Mew, bridling up.

And it almost looked as if they were going to have one of their old quarrels.   But, in a moment or two, Mew-Mew, who had a point to gain, con-trolled her temper.

" I should like, before we set out, to make one or two little preparations, dear So-Fat," she said.   " In a great undertaking like this, we should not act with too much haste.   A good sleep to-night, I should say, and the greater part of to-morrow ——."

" Well, well; as you please," interrupted So-Fat,

who was, indeed, rather sleepy himself.   " And what should you say to an extra meal ?"

" Certainly !" answered Mew-Mew.   " Leave that to me."

" Then we start to-morrow," said So-Fat.

" To-morrow, at dusk," replied Mew-Mew.

" Agreed !" said So-Fat.

Then they curled themselves up side by side upon their rug, and were both asleep in five minutes.

It all went next day as they had proposed. They slept throughout the morning, only rousing themselves to take their breakfasts.   In the afternoon So-Fat went to take a farewell walk round the farm-yard, and Mew-Mew busied herself in stealing a roast chicken out of the larder, and conveying it to a safe place in the dust-bin ; then she set to work, and washed herself all over till she was as white as snow, and by dusk she was quite ready to set out. She met So-Fat by appointment at the dust-bin, where they ate the fowl between them to the last bone, and then, though they felt a little heavy after their meal, and not quite so ready for a walk as they had expected to be, they made their way to the gate of the farm, and stepped out into the road.

" Now we've done it !" said So-Fat, as they found themselves fairly in the highway.

" Yes, we've done it," answered Mew-Mew,

rather falteringly, not finding herself quite so comfortable either in mind or in body as she could have wished.

"We must step out briskly," said So-Fat, "for I dare say they'll be after us in half an hour."

"Oh, as briskly as you please," answered Mew-Mew, almost wishing she was back at the kitchen fire.

"Now then!" said So-Fat.

And off they started at full speed.

———>—•—•—•—<———

"Oh, go on! A. Z., go on!" cried Gracie, when A. Z. stopped.

Gracie had been sitting on a stool at A. Z.'s feet ever since the story began, not doing a single thing but looking into her face. It was a story quite after Gracie's heart.

"But I can't go on any more to day, Gracie," said A. Z. "I'm tired."

"Oh!" Gracie couldn't see how anybody could get tired of talking about dogs and cats.

"You might make it short, and finish it off, A. Z.," said Tom, bluntly.

"Oh, Tom!" cried Gracie, piteously.

"Well, for that matter, Gracie," answered A. Z., "I could finish it off quite easily in half a minute,

if anybody wanted it.   For, you know, there are
two ways (at the least) of telling a story; you may
give only the dry bones, or you may give the bones
with the meat on them, just as you please.   Now, I
am quite willing to give you either."

"Oh, then, give me the bones and the meat too,"
cried little Gracie, laughing.

"I don't think the dry bones would be much
worth having, would they, A. Z.?" asked Dick.

"I'm afraid they wouldn't, Dick.   Not *my* dry
bones, at any rate," answered A. Z.   "Only Tom
wants them."

"Oh, *I* don't want them particularly," mumbled
Tom, half sheepishly.   "Only you see it's all such
nonsense, A. Z."

"About So-Fat and Mew-Mew, Tom?"

"Yes; making them say and do such absurd
things."

"Well, it *is* nonsense," answered A. Z., confidentially.   "What do you think is the use of it,
Tom?"

"The use of it?" echoed Tom, opening his eyes.
Tom had a suspicion that he didn't quite understand
what A. Z. would be at.

"Yes; the use of it?" repeated A. Z., quite
gravely.

"Why, there's *no* use in it!" exclaimed Tom.

"Nor in any story, is there, Tom?" asked A. Z.

"There's a use in sensible stories," answered Tom a little uneasily. "I mean in nice stories about real things."

"What kind of use?" inquired A. Z.

"I mean — they amuse people — they — why, *every* body likes good stories. *I* can't begin to explain the use of them," said Tom uncomfortably. "I don't know why you're asking all these things of *me*."

"Because you objected to my story being nonsense," answered A. Z. "Now, if a sensible story is useful because it amuses *you*, Tom, why should not a *non*sensical one be useful, too, if it amuses Gracie?"

"Oh, but Gracie's such an atom of a thing!" cried Tom.

"So she is, Tom," answered A. Z. "But, then, if we did nothing for all these little atoms, what do you think would become of them?"

Well, Tom had nothing to say in reply to that question, so he only made a very queer kind of voice quite down at the bottom of his throat, which *might* have been words, only they were so far off that nobody could hear them; and then, wheeling right round—

"I did not say that *I* did not like your story, A. Z.," he said, in rather a shame-faced way—for the fact was that he had both listened and laughed while A. Z. had been telling it, and, being an honest boy, his conscience was beginning to prick him for pretending that he thought it all so very much beneath him.

"Oh!" exclaimed A. Z. "Perhaps it's Dick, then, that does not like it?"

But Dick laughed, and said he had no objection to it at all.

"Or Frank?" said A. Z. "Or—suppose whoever can stand no more of it holds up a hand!"

There were no hands held up, however, and the children all laughed, and said they would rather hear the end of the story than not.

"Well, then, I think, for Gracie's sake," said A. Z., "we must finish it. So we'll have the rest to-morrow."

In spite of it being such a foolish story, all the six children came next afternoon into the parlour to hear the adventures of So-Fat and Mew-Mew. Gracie established herself again on her stool at A. Z.'s feet, and resigned herself to blissful enjoyment. The rest took their seats as they pleased, and A. Z. began.

ADVENTURES OF SO-FAT AND MEW-MEW.

PART THE SECOND.

"I DARESAY they'll be after us in half an hour," So-Fat had said; and, under that belief (for, undervalued as they certainly were, yet it was quite impossible, both So-Fat and Mew-Mew thought, that more than a very short time could elapse before the news of their disappearance would spread anxiety and alarm throughout the farm), they started off upon their journey at a speed which very soon made poor Mew-Mew quite breathless. Mew-Mew could run very fast for a little way, but she was not at all accustomed to long races, and she had not run for half a mile when the unusual exercise, joined to the large meal that she had eaten before setting out, began to make her feel quite ill. "It's fine fun—isn't it, Mew-Mew?" So-Fat had called out in high glee

more than once, for So-Fat was quite used to fast
running, and did not mind it a bit; and Mew-Mew
had panted—"Oh yes, delightful!" two or three
times, in answer to him; but at last, when for about
the sixth time So-Fat shouted—"Oh, isn't it fun?"
instead of answering as before, Mew-Mew gasped
out —" Yes — yes — it's — certainly — fun, — but —
could not we—just—just—just—rest a little,—So-
Fat?"

"What—rest already?" cried So-Fat.

"Yes — just — for — a — minute," panted Mew-
Mew.

"Oh, well, certainly, if you wish it," answered
So-Fat, a little offended, and standing still. "But
what's the matter with you? Have you got a bone
in your throat?"

"Oh no,—not—not a bone," answered Mew-
Mew, laying her paw over her chest and panting.
"It's only—only my lungs, So-Fat."

"What's the matter with your lungs?" asked
So-Fat.

"Delicate," answered Mew-Mew, shaking her
head.

"Oh, that's awkward," said So-Fat. "I don't
see how you're to move much about the world unless
you've good lungs."

"But we are not always—to be running—are

we, So-Fat?" cried Mew-Mew, with quite a wild look in her eyes.

"Well, no, not quite always," answered So-Fat. "But there will be a good deal of it. It's very awkward indeed."

"But it can't be helped, dear So-Fat," said Mew-Mew, timidly.

"No, I suppose it can't," replied So-Fat, slowly. "We must just make the best of it. Are you ready now, Mew-Mew?"

"Oh yes," answered Mew-Mew, getting on her legs again. "Only—if you think we *could* go a little slower now."

"Well, if they catch us you know it won't be *my* fault," said So-Fat, shrugging his shoulders.

And off they started again.

But though they did go slower, and though they stopped several times again to rest, it was still a very fatiguing evening to poor Mew-Mew. It was distressing to her, too, in more ways than one; for not only was she tired and out of breath, but her beautiful white paws were all so discoloured by dust and mud that she was perfectly wretched when she looked at them, not to mention that the soles of them were so swollen that she could scarcely walk.

"Oh, dear me, how shall I ever get them clean again!" cried poor Mew-Mew to herself a dozen times over, and she limped on slower and slower till at last she could scarcely even limp at all.

"Well, I *did* think you had been a better runner than this, Mew-Mew," said So-Fat, not in a very sweet temper, when he found she could not go a step further.

"Oh! I shall be better to-morrow," answered Mew-Mew, with a sickly smile. "It's only—it's only my paws. Oh, So-Fat, do *you* never suffer from your paws?"

"Suffer from them!" echoed So-Fat in a fright. "No!"

"Well, I wonder you don't. Just look at mine," said Mew-Mew.

And they did look odd certainly, for they were near twice their common size, and as black as the ground.

"Why, they're swollen up as if you had thorns in them," said So-Fat. "You ought to put them into water and bathe them."

"Put my paws into water!" cried Mew-Mew blazing up. "I would not do such a thing for the world!"

"What do you mean to do with them, then?" asked So-Fat.

"I mean to lick them," answered Mew-Mew, with dignity.

" Well, it will take a pretty time to lick *those* paws clean," said So-Fat. " However, if you *mean* to do it, you'd better begin, for I suppose we shan't go much further to-night. You won't mind if I go to sleep, will you, Mew-Mew ? "

" Oh dear, no ! " answered Mew-Mew, civilly.

" I could eat a morsel of supper," said So-Fat wistfully; " but I suppose there's not likely to be anything quite at hand ? "

" Well, no," said Mew-Mew carelessly, not having quite recovered from her last meal yet ; " I don't think there is."

" Oh, it's not of much consequence," answered So-Fat, rather dolefully. And, with a sigh, he curled himself up, and, in spite of going without his supper, he was asleep in two minutes.

As for poor Mew-Mew, she had two hours good work before she could follow his example. She licked, and licked, and licked, and it seemed as if she should never get herself white again ; but at last, to her exquisite delight, the old beautiful colour did come back, and with a gentle sigh of content- ment she rolled herself up into a ball, and fell so sound asleep that she never awoke once till morning.

She would have been glad enough, too, I dare say, to have slept for half the next day, if So-Fat would have let her, but the sun had scarcely risen when he came and roused her.

"Up, up!—awake, Mew-Mew!" he cried, bustling about and frisking round her, and Mew-Mew had to jump up, and do the best she could to get her sleepy eyes open.

"No time to lose!" cried So-Fat, as brisk as possible. "What are we to do for breakfast? Come; think, Mew-Mew!"

"Oh, we'll have some birds," said Mew-Mew sleepily. "Just wait a minute or two, So-Fat, till I've w-w——"

"Till I've washed myself," Mew-Mew had been going to say, but before she had got the last words out, all at once she heard such a twittering in the trees above her that it quite put them out of her head, and looking up to see what the cause of it was—

"Oh!" she cried, springing to her feet, "look at the birds! Oh dear me, So-Fat, look at the birds! Oh, look at them! look at them!" cried Mew-Mew, getting so excited that she scarcely knew what she was saying—for she had never seen so many birds all together in her life before.

"Well, I see them," answered So-Fat, a little irritably—for birds were rather a sore subject with So-Fat. (The truth was, that he never could manage to catch a bird himself, while Mew-Mew was remarkably clever at getting them, and the sight of the

K

delicious morsels which she used, by laying in wait for them, constantly to procure for herself, had really of old been more than So-Fat had been able to bear.) "I see them," answered So-Fat; "but I wish you'd catch a few, without saying so much about it."

"Oh, I'll catch them!" replied Mew-Mew, all alive. And she lost no time about it, for she got a couple of poor little sparrows to begin with, in less than two minutes.

As soon as ever So-Fat had tasted them he got into good humour again.

"Very finely flavoured birds," said So-Fat.

"Oh, delicious!" cried Mew-Mew. "Are you ready for another one, So-Fat?"

"Well, if it was not troubling you too much, dear Mew-Mew," said So-Fat.

"Oh, don't mention it!" cried Mew-Mew. "It's a pleasure!"

And she set herself to catch some more with such eagerness that it was impossible to doubt that it was.

They ate three birds a-piece, and then, being quite unable to eat any more, they lay down for a little while to recover themselves.

"It's rather warm work," said Mew-Mew, laying herself out at full length. "I wish I'd a little milk."

"Milk! Oh, you'll have to do without milk," said So-Fat, carelessly.

"To do without *milk!*" cried Mew-Mew, start-ing to her feet in a terrible fright.

"There's plenty of water," said So-Fat.

"I would not touch a drop of water to save my life!" said Mew-Mew, indignantly.

"Well, well," said So-Fat, seeing that all the hair on her back was standing on end, "we'll try and find some milk as we go along. But, in the mean-time, I want to speak to you about something else. I've been thinking, dear Mew-Mew, that, as you catch birds so charmingly, I could not do better than leave the care of our meals entirely to you. You manage all that sort of thing so well."

"I'm sure if I can please *you*, dear So-Fat," said Mew-Mew, recovering her temper, and looking quite delighted, "I shall be only too happy to undertake the charge."

"Then that is a settled point," returned So-Fat. "Everything else I'll take upon myself—the direc-tion of our journey, I mean, you know—and all that sort of thing; and in all matters of difficulty, of course, dear Mew-Mew, you must always come to me."

"I will," said Mew-Mew, tenderly.

"And now let us set off," said So-Fat.

"Certainly," replied Mew-Mew. "And perhaps we may find some milk as we go along."

So they set out.

They went on for a long way, walking mostly through fields and woods, and in quiet places where there were very few people likely to be stirring. " We had better keep away from the highroads lest we should be recognized," said So-Fat; and they managed so well that they walked on the whole morning without seeing a single creature. But at last, at a moment when they were so much engaged in talking together that they had forgotten to look ahead, suddenly they heard a tremendous sound of barking, and when, in a great fright, they turned round, there they saw an enormous shepherd dog racing after them as if he would break his neck.

" Oh!" cried So-Fat.

And—

" OH—H!" screamed Mew-Mew.

And for an instant they didn't know what on earth to do.

" We must run up a tree!" cried Mew-Mew.

" *I* can't run up a tree!" shrieked So-Fat.

" Well, I'm sure *I* can't help it," cried Mew-Mew; and away she scampered with all her might. Fortunately, there was a good large tree pretty close at hand, so she flew up it, and in a few moments was quite hidden amongst the branches.

But there was no help at hand for poor So-Fat.

SO-FAT AND MEW-MEW IN A FRIGHT.

Page 132.

Up came the great dog, roaring out—"Who are you?" and before little So-Fat could so much as answer that question, he fell upon him, and in a moment had him rolling over and over on the ground.

"Oh, Mew-Mew!" cried poor So-Fat, piteously, calling upon the only friend he had.

"What do you mean by 'Mew-Mew,' you little fool?" cried the big dog, seizing him by the nape of the neck, and giving him a shake as if he would shake his life out.

(And Mew-Mew, up in the tree, you may be sure, sat as still as a mouse.)

"Oh, let me go, and I'll never—never—n-e-ver," cried So-Fat, with his voice getting fainter and fainter at each word, for the great dog had got him fairly round the throat now, and So-Fat had not breath enough left to get out what it was that he would never do. "It's all over with me!" thought poor So-Fat; and he shut his eyes, and gave himself up for lost.

But at this very moment a great loud voice came roaring over the field.

"Come off, Cæsar! Whew!—do you hear? Come off, lad!" cried the voice, and the big dog at the sound lifted up his head, and, though he still held him pinned fast to the ground, yet So-Fat was able to take a great new breath.

"Come off, you rascal!" the voice shouted afresh. and it went shouting over and over again in the same way, till at last, after slowly and slowly loosening his hold, the big dog stooped down, and gave one last terrible shake to poor little So-Fat, and then, springing away, bounded across the field, and in half-a-dozen seconds was out of sight.

Then, as soon as he was quite gone, So-Fat, who had been in too dreadful a fright for some moments to open his lips, began to groan with all his might.

"Oh!" said So-Fat. "Oh! Oh!"

And they were such dismal groans that they quite made Mew-Mew's heart, as she sat upon the tree, come into her mouth.

"What shall I do? Shall I come down, So-Fat?" cried Mew-Mew, in great alarm.

But So-Fat pretended not to hear, and went on groaning harder than ever.

"Oh, dear, dear, I do think he's dying!" cried Mew-Mew; and at that dreadful thought down she came, though she was trembling so that she could scarcely stand.

"So-Fat! can you speak?" she called out, as soon as ever she got to the ground.

"Away! Leave me!" said So-Fat, in a feeble tone.

"Leave you? Never!" cried Mew-Mew, all in

a flutter, and, giving a careful glance all round her, she came up eagerly to where So-Fat lay.

"Oh, my poor dear, *dear* So-Fat! Why, you're beaten into a jelly!" cried Mew-Mew.

"If *I'm* beaten into a jelly, *you're* safe enough at any rate," said So-Fat, with a dreadful look.

"Ah, yes! And isn't it a mercy that I am?" asked Mew-Mew, looking as simple as a new-born kitten. "I wonder who would nurse you now if *I* wasn't safe!"

There was something in that; so, though So-Fat still felt angry enough, he thought he had better hold his tongue and say no more about it. Accordingly, he swallowed his wrath, and when Mew-Mew began to run over all the things that she could do for him, and suggested first putting him to bed, and then getting some water for him, and then killing a bird, he condescended to say that perhaps he *might* be the better for a little morsel of food, and that, if a very fine bird were brought to him, he *would* try if he could take a few mouthfuls of it. So away Mew-Mew went to find a bird for his dinner.

But go where she would, up and down, not a bird could Mew-Mew get. They were in a very open country, with only a few trees scattered here and there, and not a bird seemed to be in the place. It was in vain that Mew-Mew ran up the trees, and crept along the branches, and prowled about on the ground; she only saw about half-a-dozen birds in the course of a whole hour, and not one of these half-dozen could she catch.

At last she returned to So-Fat quite dejected and worn out.

"Well, I thought you were never coming back," exclaimed So-Fat, as soon as he saw her. "Come, make haste! Where are the birds?"

"Oh, So-Fat!" cried Mew-Mew, "I can't find any!"

"You can't find any birds!" exclaimed So-Fat, in dismay.

"Not one!" cried Mew-Mew, bursting into tears.

"Well, here's a pretty business!" said So-Fat.

"It's the most wretched, miserable place I ever was in!" cried Mew-Mew, and began to sob as if her heart would break.

"You ought to have managed better, Mew-Mew," said So-Fat, severely. "It's *your* part to provide food; I told you so."

"And it's *your* part to take care of us on the way, and you've done *that* nicely, haven't you?" said Mew-Mew, firing up.

"*You've* got very little to complain of, any way!" answered So-Fat, spitefully.

"If I haven't, it's no thanks to you!" retorted Mew-Mew.

And then they set to, and had a regular quarrel, and I dare say they might even have come to blows if it had not been that So-Fat was so much disabled that anything more at present in the way of fighting was quite out of the question for him. So, instead of fighting, after they had snapped at one another for a quarter of an hour or so, they ended by making it up again, and, as poor So-Fat felt very ill and shaken and uncomfortable, and could travel no further to-day, and as there was clearly no food to be had, for want of anything better to do they rolled themselves up into a couple of as tight balls as they could, for it was rather cold, and soon fell fast asleep.

They slept all the rest of the day, and, though by night time they were very hungry, they would probably have slept all night too, had it not been that an hour or two after it got dark a dreadful pelting storm of rain began. Mew-Mew was the first whom it awakened, and she sat up and looked about her, and was almost out of her wits with fright when she saw what was going on.

"So Fat! So-Fat! it's raining!" cried Mew-Mew.

"Well," said So-Fat, looking up very sleepily, "pray don't make such a noise about it. I can't help it."

"But it's *pouring* with rain!" cried Mew-Mew. "What shall I do! I shall be drowned!"

"Oh, stuff!" answered So-Fat. "Creep closer under the hedge, and be quiet." And So-Fat curled his tail warmly again over his face.

But Mew-Mew was in far too great a state of consternation to be quiet. When So-Fat wouldn't attend to her, she began to run backwards and forwards, shaking her paws, and setting up the fur on her back, and howling so dreadfully that it was quite impossible for So-Fat to get another wink of sleep. And, indeed, before many minutes were over, So-Fat himself began to get so wet that he didn't more than half like it, and, fairly giving up all hope of going to sleep again, he got up, and began to shake himself almost as vigorously as Mew-Mew.

"It's very awkward," said So-Fat, presently.

"Awkward!" echoed Mew-Mew, indignantly. "It's TERRIBLE!" And then she gave such a frightful howl that you might have heard it a mile off.

"Well, I'm sure, Mew-Mew," said So-Fat, in great distress, "I'm as sorry as you are. But who *could* have supposed that it was going to rain to-night?"

"Oh, *I* don't know who could have supposed it," answered Mew-Mew. "It was *your* business to find out that."

"I'm sure I don't know what I could have done if I *had* found it out," answered poor So-Fat, feeling quite subdued.

But Mew-Mew was not in any humour to be satisfied with excuses. She was so wretched she did not know what to do. She never had been wet in all her life before, and now she was wet, and cold, and hungry, and sleepy all together ; and, worst of all, every bit of white was gone out of her beautiful coat. "To think that I should ever live to be such an object as this," cried poor Mew-Mew. And then she began to howl again till all the place rang.

"I wish I never, never, never had come away from home!" said Mew-Mew, bursting into tears.

"Well, I'm sure, Mew-Mew, we did it for the best," said So-Fat, dolefully. "And if only the rain would stop, and we could get a little food"—And then poor So-Fat gave a dismal sigh, and such a vision rose before him of the regular meals and the warm, comfortable kitchen at home, that his voice quite broke down, and he could not utter another word.

Well, it was a wretched business. The rain fell straight on the whole night through, and when morning came, you never saw two more pitiable objects than were poor little So-Fat and Mew-Mew— Mew-Mew especially. She looked as if she had been dragged through the sea. Every hair of her white coat was dripping wet, and she was shaking so in every limb that she could scarcely stand. It would have made your heart bleed, Gracie [said A. Z.], to see her.

The morning did come, however, at last, and when the sun rose the rain ceased.

" Now, if only the ground were not so wet," said So-Fat, quite worn out, " I think I could go to sleep."

" Ah, there's no sleep for *me !*" said Mew-Mew, dolefully.

" Dear me, why not ?" asked So-Fat, quite with anxiety.

" Do you think I could go to sleep looking *this* figure ? " cried Mew-Mew, and with a shudder she raised one of her front paws and began to give it a few hopeless licks.

" Oh, that's what you mean, is it ?" said So-Fat; and, knowing that it was no use to say another word, he shrugged his shoulders, and laid himself down in the driest place that he could find, and composed himself to sleep.

But before he had slept half as long as he felt inclined to do, he was awakened by the most dreadful groans from Mew-Mew.

" Oh ! Oh ! Oh, So-Fat !" panted Mew-Mew.

" What ever is the matter now ?" cried So-Fat, lifting up his head.

There was Mew-Mew sitting before him, with

one half of her washed quite white, and the other half still all draggled and wet—the oddest looking object you can conceive, and with such a dismal look in her face, too, that it quite gave So-Fat a turn when he saw her.

"Oh, So-Fat, I'm so ill!" cried Mew-Mew.

"Dear me, you *do* look queer!" said So-Fat, rousing himself and staring at her.

"Yes; I'm so ill," repeated Mew-Mew, waggling her head, and looking very odd indeed. "I'm so ill, dear So-Fat. I'm so ill—I'm so ill!"

"Bless me, you need not say it so often!" cried So-Fat, quite excited. "Why, what's the matter with you?"

"Oh, *I* don't know," answered Mew-Mew. "But I'm so ill—I'm so ill." And off she went again just in the same way.

Upon that So-Fat was very much alarmed, and got up and felt her pulse, and found that she was in a high fever.

"Well, here's a pretty to do!" said So-Fat.

"Oh, *do* fetch me a little milk! I'm so thirsty," cried Mew-Mew.

"Milk! Where am *I* to get milk from?" exclaimed So-Fat.

"Go to the dairy-maid, and she'll give you some. She's just gone into the dairy with a great pail of milk. I've been trying for ever so long to get in, too, and taste the cream, but I can't get the door open. There!—it's open now! Oh, run in—run in—run in, So-Fat!" cried poor little Mew-Mew, as fast as ever she could gabble.

It put So-Fat in such a fright to hear her that he did not know what on earth to do.

"She's going mad!" whispered So-Fat to himself, and he began to shake so that he could not utter another word.

"Oh, the milk—the milk, So-Fat!" cried Mew-Mew. "Why didn't you run in when I told you? The door's shut again now, and you can't get in—it's no use, you can't. All the mice will have it to themselves now. There they go! There they go!" And Mew-Mew tossed up her front paws in the air, and was so weak when she had done that that she fairly fell backwards, and could not lift herself up again.

Of course it was quite impossible for them to go on with their journey that day. Mew-Mew did not know what she was either doing or saying (for this dreadful wetting that she had undergone had been too much for her), and as for strength, she had no more than a new-born kitten.

"It's the most unfortunate thing I ever knew in my life!" cried So-Fat, wringing his paws ; and once for a moment he thought of going on by himself and leaving Mew-Mew to her fate, but when he looked at her, and remembered how fond he was of her, and she of him, he had not the heart to do that. " But *I must* have something to eat, at any rate," said So-Fat, "or I shall die." So he presently left Mew-Mew dozing on the ground, and went away to look for some food.

After the greatest exertion he did succeed in catching one single bird. It was only a very small thin bird, but he gobbled it up, bones and feathers and all, and, wretched though this breakfast was, he comforted himself a little by the thought that, at any rate, he was better off than Mew-Mew, who had not any breakfast at all. So, after looking well in all directions, and seeing that there was no present chance of any more food, he went back to where he had left Mew-Mew, and, seeing that she was not a bit better, but rather, on the contrary, decidedly worse—for she scarcely seemed to know who So-Fat was when he came to her, and would do nothing but go rambling on about mice, and ducks, and chickens, and all the other things that she had left in the farm behind her—he rolled himself up and went off to sleep, as the best way of forgetting his troubles.

I can't describe to you, Gracie [said A. Z.], every incident of this day and of the days that followed, because if I did I don't know when my story would come to an end; but they were very deplorable days indeed. Poor little Mew-Mew lay on the ground so ill that she could scarcely lift up her head, and So Fat was almost starved. He managed, with the greatest difficulty to catch one or two birds a day, but these were only just enough to keep him alive, and his poor little bones soon began to look as if they would start through his skin. As for Mew-Mew, *she* never ate anything at all, and So-Fat could not for the life of him make out how it was that she was not dead, and was terrified to ask, lest it should put it into her head to want something. "And I'm sure I've nothing to give her," said So-Fat. "I've little enough for myself."

But poor Mew-Mew never asked for anything, except a little milk (which she never got), and day after day she lay on the damp ground, with all her pretty coat soiled and draggled and ruffled, talking away to herself about the ducks and the geese, and actually two or three times taking So-Fat himself for a chicken or a pig, and setting up her back at him. "She's quite wrong in her head," said So-Fat; and she certainly was.

But the longest lane has a turning, and cats, as everybody knows, have nine lives, so, after more than a week had passed, to the great surprise of So-Fat, who was fully expecting her death, Mew-Mew began to get better.   On the tenth day after she had been taken ill she sat up for an hour, and feebly expressed a desire for something to eat.

"Oh, I should so like a little piece of fish!" said Mew-Mew.

"Fish!" exclaimed So-Fat, quite aghast; "where ever do you expect to find fish here?"

"Oh, I don't know," answered Mew-Mew, faintly; "but I *should* so like a little piece."

"I only wish you'd go and get it, then," said So-Fat, quite excited; "if you had said a bird, now, I *could* have gone and looked for one; though such a wretched place as this for birds, and everything else, I never saw; but fish!—I couldn't find a bit of fish to save my life."

"There was plenty of fish at home," said Mew-Mew, dolefully, after a deep pause.

"So there was; and mice.   Do you remember the mice in the kitchen?" asked So-Fat, gloomily.

"Remember them! ah!" said Mew-Mew; "and the boiled chickens!"

"Yes; and the ducks," exclaimed So-Fat.

"I wonder what they're having for dinner to-day," said Mew-Mew, in a sad voice.

"Ah, I wish I knew!" cried So-Fat.

"You'd fetch me some of it,—wouldn't you, dear So-Fat?" asked Mew-Mew.

"I'd fetch *myself* some of it—I know that," answered So-Fat; "I don't think it would be good for you, Mew-Mew."

"Well, perhaps it wouldn't," said Mew-Mew, with a deep sigh; "but, oh, So-Fat, what are we to do?"

Well, So-Fat couldn't tell what they were to do a bit; he only knew that he was so hungry, and so cold and miserable, that he wished—and then he began to sob—he wished that he and Mew-Mew were both dead; for, as to getting any food in this wretched place, he believed he had eaten up already every bird that there was in it; and, if Mew-Mew were to be fed now as well as himself, he didn't know what ever was to come of it. So then they both sat silent, and looked dolefully in each other's face.

"I'm sure I should never, never, have come away from home if it hadn't been for you, So-Fat," said Mew-Mew, at last.

"And if it hadn't been for your good, I'm sure *I* should never have thought of leaving," answered So-Fat. "It's very ungrateful of you to speak in that way, Mew-Mew." And So-Fat burst into tears.

"I'm sure I don't want to be ungrateful," returned Mew-Mew, crying too; "but if you knew how ill I am;" and then Mew-Mew began to sob so, that she could say nothing more.

"And if you knew how hungry *I* am," cried So Fat; and he began to whine so dreadfully, that it was quite depressing to hear him.

"I wish we had never, never, come away," cried Mew-Mew, sobbing.

"We might go back," said So-Fat, in a feeble voice.

"We should never find our way," said Mew-Mew, dejectedly.

"We could but try," said So-Fat, faintly.

"I'm sure *I'm* not in a state to try anything," said Mew-Mew.

"Could you eat a bird if I were to catch one?" asked So-Fat, dolefully, after a pause.

"I might be able to take a mouthful," answered Mew-Mew.

"Well, it's a chance if I shall find one," answered So-Fat, and he went away with a deep sigh.

It happened, however, to-day, that he had better luck than usual; he caught a couple of birds, and, having taken the precaution of eating the first one himself, he brought the other to Mew-Mew. Mew-Mew was very weak, and couldn't eat much; but she took the breast of the bird, and gave the wings and legs to So-Fat; and then, a little comforted, they rolled themselves up and went to sleep for the night.

But both So-Fat and Mew-Mew were as nearly starved as a little dog and cat ever were during the week that came next. Mew-Mew wasn't strong enough to catch birds, and the very few that So-Fat could get scarcely sufficed to keep life in them. They wandered about the country as well as Mew-Mew was able ; but the farthest they could go was never far enough to carry them back to the woods where the birds abounded. Day after day they both got weaker and weaker. Mew-Mew could scarcely draw her poor feeble swollen paws after her ; and, though So-Fat was not quite so exhausted as she was, yet it was as much as even he could do, in prowling about for food, to walk a few miles a day. They were of course in wretched spirits ; for hours they would sit together without once opening their lips, except to groan ; or, if they did begin to speak, they were both so miserable that they were more likely than not to quarrel. Such a wretched-looking pair of objects they were, too ! So-Fat's black coat was all rusty and dusty, and almost worn into holes by his bones coming through ; and as for Mew-Mew's beautiful white fur, you would scarcely have believed that it ever could have been white at all, so soiled and torn and ruffled it was. The poor

little cat used still to wash her paws and her face two
or three times a day, but she hadn't strength to do
anything more; and a more miserable, draggle-
tailed, piteous little puss than she was you never
saw, Gracie, in all your days.

The only thing they both thought of now was
the possibility of getting home once more. One
evening, two or three days after Mew-Mew had begun to get on her legs again, as they sat together at
the foot of a tree, waiting as usual for birds, they
had fallen into a violent quarrel together—the most
dreadful quarrel they ever had. It was all about
leaving home, and who's fault it was. Mew-Mew,
of course, said that all the blame lay with So-Fat;
and So-Fat said that Mew-Mew was to the full as
bad—indeed rather worse—than he was; and then
Mew-Mew, in a great passion, said that So-Fat was
telling a lie, and that he was a nasty false cowardly
creature, and, weak though she was, upon this she
made a spring at him, and gave him such a box on
the ears, that he, being very weak too, quite tumbled
down; and then, as soon as he got on his legs again,
of course he flew at Mew-Mew; and for a minute or
two it really seemed as if they would make an end
of one another on the spot. But they hadn't
strength enough to do it; and presently poor Mew-
Mew fell back howling, and So-Fat retreated, limp-

ing upon three legs, and they sat down again opposite one another; and though they sulked, and
neither of them would speak a word to the other
for half an hour, yet at last Mew-Mew, who was
very tender-hearted, couldn't keep silence any
longer. So—

"I'm sure I didn't mean to hurt you, So-Fat,"
said Mew-Mew.

"Oh, don't talk to me!" said So-Fat, who, being
a gentleman, felt that he had his dignity to keep
up.

"But who else have I got to talk to? and I
must talk to somebody!" cried Mew-Mew.

"I don't see that at all," answered So-Fat with
great dignity.

"Well, I'm sure *I* do," said Mew-Mew. "It
would be a pretty thing," and Mew-Mew looked
quite in a flutter, "if, in addition to all, I was
obliged to hold my tongue. No, that's what I'll
never do! I know how to be quiet as well as most
people—but not to talk when I like!—that's a
thing I never will submit to. I shan't be in this
w-world much longer," said poor Mew-Mew plain-
tively, with the tears starting to her eyes. "You
may bear with me for the little longer that I have
to stay. Don't let it lie on your conscience when
I'm gone that you told me not to talk to you;"

and Mew-Mew was so much moved that she put her paws over her face and began to cry.

"Well, you needn't go on like that," said So-Fat half surlily, though he was a good deal agitated too by this appeal. "I'm sure you may talk if you like, though what good talking is to do to either of us *I* don't know. I wish we were dead," said So-Fat.

"We soon shall be," answered Mew-Mew, scarcely able to speak.

"We're not dead *yet* though, at any rate," returned So-Fat, rather sharply, for though he expressed a desire to see the end of his existence, he was not altogether prepared to relish such a ready assurance of its being close at hand.

"Well, it's as bad for us as if we were," answered Mew-Mew hopelessly. "Oh, So-Fat, why did we ever, ever, run away?"

Now Mew-Mew had often asked that question before, and So-Fat had always answered, "We did it for the best;" but to-day, instead of answering as usual, So-Fat did nothing but groan and sigh.

"We were so comfortable!" said Mew-Mew, weeping copiously.

"We were!" answered So-Fat.

"What did we know of hunger?" cried Mew-Mew. "There was always food there: breakfast, dinner, supper—when did any of them fail us?"

"Never!" said So-Fat, striking his forehead.

"Birds there were the luxuries—the superfluities of life," said Mew-Mew mournfully, rising with the grandeur of her subject, "not its necessities."

"I'm sure *I* had few enough of them," answered So-Fat, remembering that old bone of contention, "one way or another."

"Yet they were free to all," answered Mew-Mew. "Hundreds of them!—ah, hundreds and hundreds!" cried Mew-Mew in a broken voice.

"*You* always caught them easily," said So Fat gloomily.

"I did," mildly returned Mew-Mew.

And then there was a pause for several moments.

"We had warmth too," said Mew-Mew presently; "a warm fire winter and summer in the kitchen."

"It got *too* warm sometimes," said So-Fat.

"It never got too warm for me," answered Mew-Mew. "There were—some—annoyances outside the house," said Mew-Mew thoughtfully. "The chickens!"

"Yes; and the pigs," said So-Fat.

"Ducks and geese too,—and cows," said Mew-Mew. "Yet we might have borne with them. Live and let live. They were not obtrusive, So-Fat."

"Well, no," answered So-Fat slowly. "I can't

say they were. They didn't meddle with us much.
They *looked* offensive."

"They did," answered Mew-Mew ; "but it might
not have been their fault. All people haven't our
air and shape, So-Fat. They meant no harm."

"No, I don't think they did," returned So-Fat.

"Oh, So-Fat!" cried Mew-Mew.

"Oh, Mew-Mew!" said So-Fat.

And then they looked at one another with the
most piteous faces you ever saw in your life.

"We—we may get home again yet," said So-Fat
faintly.

"If we did I should die in peace," said Mew-
Mew, shutting her eyes.

But the question of questions was—in what way
did home lie ? They had rambled about in so many
directions,—now to the right hand, now to the left,
now to the north, now to the south,—that how to
find the way by which they had come first they
could no longer tell for the life of them. Not a thing
could they do but wander on, without a sign to
guide them, their poor little weak legs scarcely able
to carry them. Every day as they toiled on, going
sometimes one way, sometimes another—not knowing
in which way to continue going—they found themselves growing more and more hopeless : sometimes
when the sun rose they wouldn't have the heart to

get up at all, but would lie still, shutting their eyes, and curling themselves up tight, and trying for how long they could forget their troubles in sleep : sometimes —very often—they were so hungry that they couldn't sleep, but would sit and look in each other's face, and creep close together, in a kind of fear, not knowing what was going to come.

Other troubles pursued them too. Once they ventured into a village, thinking to find some food there, and some big school-boys caught poor starved So-Fat, and tied a kettle to his tail, and hooted him through the street, and hunted him out far over the fields,—while poor Mew-Mew, with her little weak legs, had to run for her very life. One day they came to a small stream, and Mew-Mew, who had never before let water touch her paws, had to cross it upon So-Fat's back, and very nearly got drowned in doing it, for So-Fat lost his footing on the bank, and down poor Mew-Mew fell, and had to be pulled out of the water by her two front legs. It was the most terrible of all the frights that Mew-Mew had. Another day they were threatened by a big dog, and had to lie in hiding, with their hearts going pit-a-pat, for hours. And often they went from morning to night and never tasted food, or anything but a little drop of water by the roadside. But tired, and starved, and frightened, they still toiled on. " We

can but go on till we die, So-Fat," said little Mew-
Mew. So they went on, though they never knew
the least bit in the world where they were going
to.

But at last one night came when poor little Mew-
Mew laid herself down quite straight on the ground,
and put out her four paws, and said very quietly (for
she and So-Fat were both starved into being very
quiet now)—

"I can't go any further, So-Fat. You must say
good-bye to me in the morning, and go on alone."

"Oh, Mew-Mew!" cried So-Fat, and he came to
her side, and sat down, and took one of her paws in
his, and they looked into one another's faces, and the
tears came into their eyes so fast that they could
scarcely see each other.

"*I'll* stay here if you must stay, Mew-Mew," said
So-Fat. "I'll stay here and die too."

"Oh, no! you're stronger than I am, dear So-
Fat; you may get home yet," said little Mew-Mew.

"What good would it do me to get home if you
were dead?" cried poor So-Fat; and he sobbed as if
his heart would break.

"You could tell them how hard we tried to come
home together," said Mew-Mew, faintly. "I should
like them to know how hard we tried, and how
sorry we were."

"But they will never know it," said So-Fat, hopelessly. "I shall never find them. I can't go wandering on alone. I shall lie down here and die."

And then they were too weak to go on talking longer. Feeble little Mew-Mew only spoke once again.

"Put your arm round my neck, So-Fat," said Mew-Mew. "I think I shall go to sleep now. Kiss me, dear So-Fat." And she put up her little sad thin face, and So-Fat kissed her, and then she shut her eyes, and they crept close to one another for warmth, and she fell asleep.

It was a dark cold night, and poor So-Fat, who was so hungry that he couldn't go to sleep at all, lay shivering and crying, and watching Mew-Mew's faint, faint slow breathing all the night long. Every hour he thought that she would die, but the hours passed, one after another, and she still went on breathing in the same feeble way. She was still alive when the cold dawn came, and when the sun rose.

It had been night when they had come to this place—quite dark, and misty; when morning came, what do you think that So-Fat saw?

He opened his hungry eyes when the birds began to sing, and, looking up and round him, he saw—far away, beyond the fields—the farm-house at home.

There it was, with the first sunbeams falling on it, deepening the red of the warm tile roof, and the russet of the old strong walls; there it was, with all the farm buildings grouped around it—the very stacks of hay all standing in the farm-yard, as So-Fat remembered them—every one.

The little dog started up, trembling all over, gave one great look, and then such a cry that it awakened Mew-Mew in an instant out of her feeble sleep.

"Oh, So-Fat, what is it?" cried Mew-Mew, shaking all over.

But So-Fat could give no explanations—not a word would come from So-Fat save one, as he ran round and round Mew-Mew, like a creature going wild.

"Home! Home! Home!" cried So-Fat.

Yes, it was home at last! Little Mew-Mew stood up on her four legs and saw it. There it was—the red house in the sunlight. After all their wanderings and all their folly, the little cat and dog had got back to it at last.

* * *

"Oh, A. Z., is that the end?" cried Gracie.

(Gracie's voice was quite tremulous as she spoke,

for, to tell the truth, she had been fairly crying for the last five minutes.)

"Yes, Gracie, that is the end. Haven't you had about enough of it?" asked A. Z.

No, it seemed Gracie had *not* had enough of it, for she wanted to know various other things. She wanted to know, in the first place, did little Mew-Mew really die?

"Oh no," answered A. Z. to that, "Mew-Mew got better. So-Fat ran as hard as ever he could home, and got them to open the door to him; and in half an hour after that Mew-Mew was sitting before the kitchen fire, drinking a saucer of warm milk."

"Oh, was she really?" cried Gracie.

"Yes; and So-Fat had got a pound of beef without any bones in it, and was the happiest dog in the three kingdoms."

"Oh! And then—what next, A. Z.?"

"Well, next, I think," said A. Z., "they each of them had to have a bath; and after that Mew-Mew was put to bed."

"With the blankets and sheets, A. Z.; just as So-Fat had been?"

"Yes, Gracie," said A. Z., "with the blankets and sheets, in a cradle; and So-Fat used to rock her to sleep."

"And did she ever get her white coat again, A. Z. ?" asked Kitty.

"Oh yes, Kitty," replied A. Z., "in course of time she got it whiter and furrier than ever. It was a good while before it became all that she could wish, but she washed it regularly for four hours a-day, and by the end of six months, there wasn't a cat for ten miles round who could compare with her."

"And then, A. Z.," asked Gracie, thoughtfully, "when they had both got quite well again, were they good or bad ?"

"They were good," replied A. Z. "They never forgot the lesson they had learnt, and were as good a little cat and dog as ever lived, to the ends of their lives. They had their faults—but who has not, Gracie ? When they died at last, there wasn't a dry eye in the house —everybody was so fond of them."

"Oh! And then that really is the end ?" said Gracie, sorrowfully.

"Yes, Gracie, that's the end," answered A. Z.; and rose up laughing.

"Now, Tom, on this last day I'm going to tell a story to *you*," said A. Z., after dinner next afternoon, " so come here, and sit down beside me."

Whereupon (the children having by this time quite got over their original alarm at A. Z.) Tom came with a good grace, and sat down, not by A. Z.'s side, indeed, but full in face of her, and then, having taken his place—

" What kind of a story is it to be ?" asked Tom.

" A grave story," replied A. Z. " You might guess that of course I shouldn't think of talking any nonsense to *you*, Tom." And A. Z. looked so severe and solemn that it quite frightened little Gracie.

" Now, A. Z., that's too bad!" cried Tom, and half began to laugh.

" But a grave story may be very nice, Tom," said Frank, who had advanced near to A. Z.'s chair.

" *I* think grave stories are nicest," said demure Peggy.

" Oh, I'm sure *I* don't," cried Kitty, opening her eyes wide.

" Well, if it's a nice story, I don't mind," said Tom, bravely. " Only don't make it stupid, like that other one about the painter. What's this one to be about, A. Z. ?"

" You'll hear that as soon as I begin to tell it, Tom," replied A. Z. " Are you quite ready ?"

" Wait a moment," said Tom ; and began to search in his pockets. " You won't object to my making a ship, will you, A. Z. ?"

" Oh no," replied A. Z.; " quite the reverse."

Whereupon Tom produced a knob of wood and a pocket knife, and as soon as he had opened the blade, A. Z. began her tale.

STORY THE FIFTH AND LAST.

THE TWIN BROTHERS.

THERE were once two brothers [said A. Z.
"It was not long ago—was it, A. Z.?"
asked Tom, looking up from his work.

"No; quite in these times," replied A. Z.
"My story belongs entirely to this century."

"Oh!" returned Tom, with satisfaction;
and A. Z. went on.]

Two brothers. They were twins; but they
were not, as twins so often are, like one another;
they were not the least alike, either in body or mind.
The elder, who was called George, was a quiet, grave
boy, too reserved and shy to be much of a general
favourite; but the other, whose name was Norman,
was one of the brightest, joyfulest, most light-
hearted boys you ever knew—a boy whom every-

body loved, and who was willing to love every one. He was, indeed, as these very light-hearted boys often are, rather careless and thoughtless, and was continually falling into some scrape or other—but then he was so sweet-tempered and good-natured, and such a fine handsome little fellow, that nobody had the heart to be angry with him for half an hour together. Nobody, at least, except *one*. There was one person in the world who did not love Norman— and that one was his twin brother George.

It was a long time before anybody knew that George did not like his brother. When they were quite little things they had got on very well together; they had lived together in their nursery, and played together, and learnt their A B C out of the same book, and were very fair friends; but from the time they were about six years old there had been a cloud between them. It was not Norman's fault; *he* would have been friends with George, as he would with all the rest of the world, but George would not let him. The lad could not do a thing so as to please George; the more pleasant he was in the eyes of everybody else, the more he only seemed to set George against him. Yet the elder brother was so reserved, and said so little, that for a long time it was not plain to anybody—not even to Norman himself—that George did not love him.

It came at last to be found out in this way.

In the town near which they lived there was held a great annual fair, to which all the young people for miles round used to look forward as to the most important event of the year. To George and Norman, however, its delights only came in alternate years, for they lived at some distance from the town, and the chaise in which they drove by their father's side to the scene of their blissful pleasures had not space enough in it to contain them both at once. So they used to go year about. But one year when it was George's turn to go, on the very morning of the fair day, he chanced to be ailing with some slight cold; on that same morning, too, some one of Norman's many friends had presented him with a glittering new crown piece. "To spend at the fair," the giver of it said.

"Oh; but I'm afraid I'm not going to the fair!" cried Norman; and with that sped in all haste home to see what could be done.

"Oh, mother dear," he cried, having got to his mother's presence breathless, "Mr. So-and-So has given me a crown; and how *am* I to spend it unless I go to the fair?"

"I'm sure I don't know, my dear boy," answered the mother; "unless you were to go instead of George. And, indeed, I almost think it would be better, for poor George isn't very well to-day."

" Isn't he ?   Oh, then, I'll go, George!" cried Norman, clapping his hands.   And nobody said " No."

" George, my dear, you shall go next time," said his mother, and began to busy herself about her household concerns.

" Give Norman your half-crown, and he shall spend it for you.   Perhaps some one will give *you* a five-shilling piece next fair day, my lad," said the father ; and turned to his newspaper.

Without a word, George got up from where he was sitting, and left the room.   Nobody looked at him or noticed him.   The boy went away, and nobody thought of him again till the chaise was at the door, and Norman and his father were prepared to start.   Then Norman bethought him that he had not got George's directions as to what he was to buy for him, and, rushing upstairs, began to shout— " George, where's your half-crown ?   George !   I say—George !"—all over the house.

But there was no answer to his call till he got to the door of George's little room, and, finding that, to his amazement, locked, began to kick the panels for admission.

" I say, what ever do you lock the door for ? Can't you open it ?" cried Norman.

Upon which George opened it ; and next moment a strange sound reached the ears of the mother downstairs. When she hurried up, she found George with his hands grasping his brother's shoulders, shaking him with the fierceness of a wild animal.

"George!" she cried, in great anger, and rushed forward and struck the lad.

He raised his face and looked at her; then never said a word, but loosed his hold, and went back into his room, slamming the door.

Poor Norman stood on the landing, breathless and panting.

"My dear boy! my poor, dear boy!" cried the mother, and began to caress him and speak bitterly of his brother's unkindness.

"I think he was vexed about the fair, mother," said Norman; and went downstairs very quiet.

In a minute more he was seated by his father's side, and the chaise drove away from the door.

"I must go and punish that boy," thought the mother then, and she went sadly again upstairs; but she paused when she reached the landing outside her son's room, for there was a sound of such bitter sobbing coming through the door. It was not merely the sobbing of anger—there was something more in it than that: it was a wilder and more despairing kind of weeping—a bitter hopeless wail, as though the lad's heart were breaking. The mother stood still with a strange feeling coming over her for some moments; then she put her hand to the door—it was not locked this time—and she turned the handle and went in.

The boy was lying on his face upon his bed, and did not see her till she stood beside him.

"George!" she said.

She put her hand upon his arm, and he started up with all his face on fire.

"George, why are you lying here, sobbing in this way?" she said. "You can't surely be such a baby as to cry like this merely because your brother has been taken to the fair instead of you?"

She was really sorry for her boy, and yet she spoke reprovingly, and almost harshly. If she had let him see that she was more grieved than angry— if she had spoken one gentle or loving word to him —he would have thrown his arms about her neck, and opened his heart to her; but her cold tone turned him to stone. She loved Norman's little finger more than she loved *his* whole body; it was the same with his father—the same with everybody. They were all against him. What did it matter what became of him? He thought this, and rose up silent and sullen.

"I'm very much displeased with you," the mother said again in a sad voice. "You have a violent, envious temper, George. None but a bad, cowardly boy would have attacked his brother as you did Norman just now. I wish I knew what to do with you. You don't seem to me as if you had natural affection either for him, or for your father, or me." And the mother sighed.

She might have seen the boy's lip quivering if she had looked at him—but she did not look, and he said nothing.

"You must stay in your room this evening. I can't have you amongst us," she said. "You force me to punish you, George."

"If it was Norman you would not punish *him*," the boy said, bitterly. Those were the only words he spoke.

"I would punish whichever of you did wrong," the mother answered, and then left the room.

Nobody saw George for the rest of that day. He went out as soon as his mother left him, and did not come in again till night. Norman's voice was heard clear and merry in the drawing-room as, on his return at last, he passed the door, and went up alone to his room and crept to bed. The servant who let him in said with a laugh, in the kitchen, that "Master George was sulky;" nobody saw the bitter tears that wetted the lad's pillow before he went to sleep.

Next day things went on again outwardly much as usual. George, indeed, was a degree quieter even than ordinary; and Norman for an hour or two looked shy of him. That was all that appeared; but the mother had a long grave talk alone with her husband; and from that day it was sadly acknowledged by them both that their eldest son was jealous of his brother.

"He must be watched," the father said; and henceforward he *was* watched.

But he was not a boy to be made the better by watching; he soon knew that he was suspected, and whatever bitter feelings he had had before towards Norman were only made the bitterer by discovering that. He said nothing—made no complaints, but a sharp and angry sense of injustice and unkindness sprang up in him. Before his parents he could not dare to shew his bitterness, but he soon began to revenge himself for his silence in their presence, by making his brother suffer when they were alone. He was a much bigger and stronger boy than Norman, and out of doors, and at school, if not at home, he made Norman feel his mastery. Norman was petted at home, but away from home George began to take a cruel satisfaction in making his tears flow. He was a good little fellow—that merry bright-haired Norman— not a coward or a tell-tale—a warm-hearted brave boy, who, as I said before, was ready to be friends with all the world;

and, being good and brave like this, he did not complain as often as another might have done of George's misdeeds; yet even he told of them sometimes, and then there were punishments and hard words for George, not undeserved, but every one of which only made the lad's heart the harder, or made it *seem* the harder; for he would never let any one know what he himself suffered, but would put on a dogged look of sullen indifference, on many a day when he could with more truth to himself have let both father and mother see that his heart was full almost to bursting with far other things than bitterness and jealousy; though there was enough, and far too much, at all times, of those too.

It was a bad time for George, and I don't know what would have been the end of it for him, if it had not been for an event which happened when he and Norman were about fourteen.

Amongst the boys at the school to which they went Norman had many friends. With George it was different; he, shy and jealous-tempered, a surly, close sort of lad, as he was called, held aloof from the greater number of his schoolfellows; he was strong enough and steady enough to make most of them respect him, and some of them even a little fear him; but very few amongst them loved him. With Norman, however, it was very different; he was a favourite with every one; he was the hero amongst all the young ones of the school; there were a dozen boys or more about him every day who thought that every thing that Norman did was good, and every word that Norman said was right.

One Monday morning a report was whispered along the forms in school hours, that one of the boys—a foremost one amongst those who looked up to Norman—had been taken ill with scarlatina. The attack had begun two days before—on Saturday morning—and the lad, they said, was not likely to recover.

He was a favourite in the school, and the boys' faces looked grave and eager as they talked of him; but on no one, perhaps, did the news fall with such a shock as upon Norman. A light-hearted boy, he was yet affectionate and sensitive more than most lads. He never, too, had had the thought of death brought so near to him as this. Only three days ago he had walked home from school by this boy's side, his arm about his neck; and now he was dying.

The thought of it haunted him all day. When school was over he shrank away from the other boys, and went his way home alone by George's side. Not that he expected sympathy from George, but he couldn't bear the rough careless talk of the other lads to-day. Yet he yearned for something more than merely silence, for when they had gone for a little way without speaking, side by side—

"I wonder if he is so *very* ill," said Norman, in a low grave voice.

"If you want to know, why don't you go and ask?" said George, shortly.

"Oh, do you think I might?" cried Norman, and brightened up.

"Why ever shouldn't you?" demanded George.

"I mean—you know—I mean, because they say that fevers are catching," Norman said.

"Catching from a house door? oh, you coward!" cried George, and burst into a contemptuous laugh.

"I'm *not* a coward!" Norman answered, with the colour flushing up. "I only meant that mamma might mind. Whatever I am, I'm not a coward!" cried Norman; and without another word, started off from his brother's side.

He went to the house where his schoolfellow lived; it was a house within grounds, and the house door stood open in the pleasant summer afternoon. One of the other children of the family saw him as he came near, and asked him in.

"I only came to ask how Fred was," Norman said.

"Oh, come in, then, and I'll tell mamma," the child answered.

And then Norman went in; he had better not have gone—he knew that—but he was stung by what George had said to him; so, half in bravado, he went.

One evening, five days afterwards, he came into the parlour where George was sitting alone, and throwing himself down face foremost on the sofa, burst into a great fit of sobbing.

George looked up startled from his book.

"What is the matter with you?" he said, after he had stared for a few moments.

He had to ask the question twice before it was answered. At last, in a broken voice, Norman sobbed out—

"He's dead."

"*Who's* dead? Fred Hamlyn?" cried George.

"Yes."

"How did you hear? Who told you?" George asked in a low voice.

"I was there," said Norman.

"What! at the house?"

"Yes; I saw him. I was there when he died. Oh, George!" cried Norman, and burst out into fresh sobbing.

"You were *in* the house? Do you mean to say that you have been going there and seeing him?" said George, suddenly; and he put his hand on

Norman's shoulder, and gave it a rough sharp
shake.

There was something in his voice that made the
other cease sobbing, and look up.

" If I have, what right have *you* to say anything
to me ? " he said.

" What do you mean by that ? "

They looked in one another's faces ; there was
anger, and a sort of startled fear in both of them.

" I should never have gone if you hadn't called
me a coward," said Norman, slowly.

" Did *I* tell you to go *in?*" George answered
sharply.

But Norman shrank back, and turned his face
again upon the pillows ; he wouldn't answer that
question.

" You know I didn't ; you know I wasn't thinking of your going in," said George, indignantly, and
went back to his place ; but yet something smote
him at the heart as he took up his book again ; he
knew as well as if his conscience had spoken out
loud in words, that it was his taunt that had made
his brother go.

He tried to read his book and forget about it,
but he couldn't. The thought of the boy that was
lying dead came between him and the printed page.
Why had Norman been so mad as to go in ?

" If he takes the fever"—George thought to himself once ; and then he turned the page sharply, and,
with his elbows on his knees, set himself to read
straight on. He was a brave boy enough, but he
felt at that moment what it was to be—what he had
called Norman.

He watched his brother through the school hours
next day. When school was over, and the boys began outside the school door to part into little groups
of twos and threes, he went up to him.

" Come home," he said.

" Well, I am coming home," Norman answered
peevishly, and shook off the hand that George had
laid upon his arm.

He had been irritable all day. What ailed him?
He had gone down in his class an hour ago, and had
lost head more than once that afternoon in a strange
sort of way; George looked at him as he moved
away home alone, and something rose into his throat.

He was so silent at all times, that it was very
rarely noticed at home when anything more than
usual lay at George's heart. Nobody noticed him
to day-—not brother, or father, or mother. He
thought once of telling his mother what he knew ;
but he had for so long left off telling his mother
anything, that he couldn't do it now.

Once in the course of the evening, having been

out of the room where the rest were sitting for half an hour, when he came back he found Norman in the act of laying his head down on the table by which he sat.

"What ails you, my dear?" his mother asked, seeing him do that.

"I don't know—my head aches," the boy answered languidly.

"You have got cold, perhaps: I think you have looked heavy all the afternoon," his mother said. "It would be better to go to bed, my dear."

"Oh, I don't care: I'll go presently," Norman answered slowly, and remained sitting with his head bent down.

In about half-an-hour they roused him and made him go. He said something irritably when he rose up—that he wished they would leave him alone, or something like that; and then went away.

The boys had separate rooms. A couple of hours later in the evening, when George went up to bed, he stole softly to Norman's door, and stood there and listened. He would have gone in, only he was ashamed. There was no sound. Norman must be sleeping, he thought; and he said to himself—"He will be all right by morning;" and tried to shake off his fear, and went back to his own bed.

But when morning came all the house knew that Norman was ill.

That day George went to school again as usual. He said nothing to any one. His brother wasn't well, he answered shortly when he was questioned. To those who asked what ailed him, he replied irritably that he didn't know, and would say nothing more. No one noticed anything more than common in the boy's look: he was too much in the habit of being reserved, and what the other lads called sulky, to attract much attention to himself to-day. He sat with his book before him, his elbows leaning on his desk, and his head between his hands: he often sat so to learn his lessons.

He went home alone: that was common with him too. As he came into the house, he asked in a sullen kind of way—

" How's Norman ?"

" He's very bad, Master George," the servant answered. " Its scarlatina."

" How do you know that?" George asked roughly.

"'The doctor says so," she answered.

He had thrown down his cap and his bag of books, and without another word he went past her. The dining-room was empty: he went in there, and stood for a long time at one of the open windows.

Half an hour afterwards, when his mother came into the room, she found him still there—standing at the window—doing nothing.

"Have you come home, George? I didn't hear you," she said.

He turned round and muttered something; then went up to the table and began to search for a book. She stood looking at him for a moment or two, and then said sadly—

"Have you nothing to ask about your brother? He is very ill, George."

"Yes; I know," the boy said huskily, and made no other reply.

"He was asking for you just now; but Dr. Hakin says we mustn't let you go into his room," she said. "Have you nothing to say to him, George?—no message for him?"

He hesitated uneasily for a moment or two, then muttered—"You can say I'm sorry;" and, turning away, took his book to the window and sat down.

The mother said nothing more; and George was left to sit and read through the long summer afternoon.

There was a watch kept up all that night in Norman's room, for he got fast worse and worse. When morning came, in the passage outside his room, as she opened the door early and came out, the mother found her eldest boy standing. He had been waiting there for her coming for half an hour, and yet his cold voice chilled her when he went up to her and asked how Norman was. She said quickly—"He is worse—much worse;" and passed him and went down stairs.

George stayed at home that day; nobody told him either to go or stay, but he remained. He sat alone in his own little room, catching the sounds that went on in the house, hearing the long hours strike one by one on the clock outside. Nobody came near the boy all day. He went down stairs at meal times, and in the evening he and his father sat alone together.

Late in the evening a sudden message came from the sick-room that Dr. Hakin must be sent for, for Norman was worse. The poor father started up, and said he would go for him. "Might *I* not go?" George asked; but his father only shook his head. An hour after that, when the physician's visit had been made, as he drove away from the house, all within it knew that their bright-hearted, joyous, loving Norman had entered the Valley of the Shadow of Death.

George knew it as he shut the door upon himself in his little room. Nobody had spoken to him since the tidings had been given: he had heard them, as he heard most things, in silence, and no one thought of him or gave any sympathy to him as he went his way alone.

Yet they might well have pitied the boy if they had known all. They *would* have pitied him, if they could have seen him as he sat down and laid his face upon his table, and burst into a bitter agony of sobbing. For all these years he had been unkind to Norman—and now Norman was dying. It seemed to him as if the whole world held nothing in it for him but that one thought.

It burnt itself into the boy's heart all the night long. When morning came, and Norman was no better, full of a passionate longing to do something—anything—he didn't care what—to shew his sorrow and repentance, he went to his father and mother, and told them (for he knew they did not know it yet) how Norman had caught the fever. The blame of what had been done was Norman's at least as much as George's, but George, as you might guess he would do from the mood in which he was now, took it almost all on his own shoulders. "He wouldn't have gone if it hadn't been for me : it was *my* fault," he said.

In a broken voice, when he had finished speaking, his mother said—"God forgive you, George !"

He looked into her face, and uttered a kind of cry of—"Mother !"

But she was too miserable to pay any heed to *him*; she turned away and left him: she had no heart in that hour for anything but her dying boy.

"It will be a lesson to you, George, for the rest of your life," his father said sternly.

The boy heard him, but he turned away and spoke no more. That one cry was the only appeal he made for pity or forgiveness.

He thought to himself, as, with his heart quivering, he went away—would Norman turn from him too? He had been forbidden to go to Norman's room, but he was in no state of mind now to care about that: he felt as though, come what might, he must see his brother. The thought that Norman might die and never speak to him again, swallowed up every other thought.

He went to his own room—his own little sanctuary, whose four walls had long been the only witnesses of all the bitterness and all the tenderness of the lad's heart—and waited there till he could go, unseen by any one, into his brother's room.

The opportunity did not come for a long time. When it came at last and he stole in, Norman was lying very still, with his eyes shut. He might have been asleep, for they did not open till George was close beside him, and then they opened with a start.

"Oh, George!" he said.

What followed neither of them could ever afterwards repeat. They only knew that some words were spoken,—which ended in George's part in a great broken sob. And that then their arms met about each other's necks, in an embrace in which all the old jealousy was forgotten and buried—all the old unkindness forgiven for ever.

I don't know whether this reconciliation had anything to do with Norman's recovery. In after years the two lads liked to think that it had, and Norman always stoutly said that he began to get better from that very hour: but we always know that imagination has a good deal to do with beliefs of this sort. Yet I think that it might perhaps at least have lent a helping hand: and this at any rate is true, that within twenty-four hours after their meeting the lad was certainly better; before another day was over he was pronounced out of danger; and long before the summer came to an end, he was trudging again each morning to school, as strong and happy as ever, by George's side.

Or, I ought rather to say, happier than ever. For the joyous, bright-natured boy had always found his brother's coldness and unkindness a hard thing to bear, and it made his whole life gladder now to know that he had found a place at last in George's heart. It had been a heart hard to win; but, once won, he held it ever after, through many a trial and many a strait, till it gave the last beat that it ever gave in this world.

You have heard how George was jealous of his brother, Tom [said A. Z.]; you shall hear something now of how he loved him.

He had as large a heart as ever was given to one of God's children; the great fault and mistake of his childhood had been that he had not known what use to make of it. Instead of loving those about him freely, he sat and brooded over the amount of love that was given to himself, until he learnt to think of nothing *but* himself, and to fancy that every kind word given to his sunny-natured brother was something taken away from what belonged to him. That's the way people grow morbid, Tom. So that it presently came to this, that the more he loved, and the more he hungered for love to be given to him, the more he suffered—and the less loveable he grew.

But he never fell back into this morbid state after Norman's illness. That opened his eyes; and from the hour when he first let himself love Norman, and knew that Norman loved him, all the world wore a new colour to him. He had plenty to put up with—plenty to bear—plenty of evil thoughts and feelings to crush down in himself after that —for Norman was loved more than he was to his life's end, and many a heart that George would have given his right hand to win was given to Norman unasked and uncared for; but the thick darkness that was driven out once was never suffered to come back again. He went bravely on his way, which was a hard way sometimes, but a noble one, and growing always nobler to the end of his life.

The two lads went out to India when they were eighteen. Norman had always wanted to be a soldier. I don't know that George's taste for the army was very strong, but his love for his brother was stronger in him now than any other feeling, so he went the way that Norman went. Their father was fortunate enough to get cadetships for them both ; they went to Addiscombe together, passed their examinations together, with pretty nearly equal credit, and went out in the same ship.

It was a sad day for the poor mother at home when they parted from her. Long before this George had learnt to look the fact, that his mother loved his brother better than she loved him, bravely in the face. He neither resented that love of her's now, nor wondered at it ; in *his* eyes, too, Norman had for years been first—fitted to be given all love, and worthy of it.

When they were going away she said—

"George, I give him into your hands. Take care of him, as you would of your own life."

And George answered—"I will; so may God help me."

He never spoke to his mother on earth again, but to the end of his life he kept that promise.

And Norman had need that he should keep it. For, with all his sunniness of nature, and with all his genuine wishes and even strivings to do right, he was one of those who often wandered off the broad highway into little side-paths on the right hand and on the left; and, in the very joyousness and careless ness of his heart, was throughout his life constantly half yielding to one or other of the many temp tations that surround a soldier's life. Everybody liked him, and he was ready to be hand in glove with every one—good and bad alike—who had a hearty welcome or a pleasant word to give him; and fell into small scrapes innumerable in consequence, which would have been *great* scrapes, many a time. if it hadn't been for George. But George stood at his side like his good angel, watching him, and guiding him, and upholding him, and loving him, through thick and thin, with as devoted a love as ever brother had for brother.

And reaping his reward too; for, though Norman opened his heart to every one, its highest place of all was for George alone. There was something in his love for him that was greater even than that for wife or child. He married, eight or nine years after they went out to India, a pretty little officer's daughter, and the marriage was a very right and a very happy one; but it was not his wife who did most to keep Norman's life straight; there was another voice that he listened to when her's would sometimes have been heard in vain.

George never married. When the lads first went out they lived together; when Norman brought his wife home, George set up house-keeping on his own account; but years afterwards they came together, and lived under one roof again. It was the happiest arrangement for them both.

After a good many years had passed, they began to talk of taking their furlough and going home. How glad, they said, the dear old mother would be! But, though they spoke of it often, yet year after year passed, and they never went. Norman sent home his children one by one to the old couple as they grew too old for the Indian climate, but he himself and George never returned. There was always some obstacle or difficulty in the way—now one thing now another—and they always said, "We will try and go next year." And then at last, before they had ever gone, the old mother died.

The brothers sat together for many an hour on the evening of the day on which they heard the news of her death. It was too late then to wish that they had broken through everything and gone home.

They should never see her again now; but the old father was still alive, and they began to plan how they would go before it was again too late, and see him. They arranged everything for their departure in the spring, and when the spring came they went. They took the long sea passage by the Cape —a happy little party of four—George, and Norman, and his wife, and their youngest child.

Three of them reached their journey's end in safety, but the fourth never set his eyes on the old English land again. When they were about half way home, a fever broke out on board, and began to commit great ravages amongst the men. Presently, the surgeon also caught it and died. There was great panic and distress on board, the passengers in terror of infection, the captain dreading that he might not preserve hands enough to work the ship home. And now the doctor was dead! Who was to attend to the sick, or try to prevent the fever spreading?

One of the passengers, an Indian officer, went to the captain, and said to him that he had studied medicine a little, and would, if he chose, do his best to supply the surgeon's place; and then he went and took up his post below. He laboured there day and night. Some more of the men died; some got over their sickness and recovered; when they were within a week of their journey's end, the fever was almost stayed.

But *one* was struck with it now who would never raise his head more; the brave heart that had lent courage to all the rest was laid low. They brought him up from his close berth and laid him on the deck. He had asked if they were near England, and his dying eyes strained across the sea in yearning for the sight of her white cliffs. But they were too far away—he never saw them.

A little group of loving faces sat round him, and he died with Norman's hand in his.

"I have been very happy. Thank God!" he said with his last breath. And then the brave heart stopped its beating.

"You have been the noblest brother and the truest friend that ever man had!" poor weeping Norman said over the quiet face.

That is all my story, Tom [said A. Z.] It ends here with George's death. Of my two brothers, Norman, you see, had the most happiness in this world; but perhaps the crown that is yet to come may be for George.

It was rather a grave story for A. Z.'s last—too grave by far for Grace and Kitty, who had little notion of anything in stories but fun and laughter. Life and the things of life were not serious matters by any means to Grace and Kitty. But the other children rather liked this last tale of A. Z.'s There were tears in Frank's bright eyes when she had finished telling it, and something in it kept the tongues of all of them quiet for a few moments after she had finished speaking.

Tom was the first to say anything. The story had been *his* story, and of course he felt that some criticism on it was called for especially from him. So—

"That George was a fine fellow," said Tom.

"And it's a true story, isn't it, A. Z.?" asked clear-eyed Frank.

"Some of it is quite true, Frankie," A. Z. answered. "And all of it, I think, *has been* true—many a time—though I have chosen my own way of putting it, you know, as story-tellers do."

"If Dick and I ever go to India and be soldiers," said Tom, thoughtfully, "I wonder if *we* shall be at all like Norman and George."

"Which of us do you mean to be Norman?" inquired Dick at that, pretty sharply. Dick had a notion that Tom meant Norman for him.

" Oh, *I* don't know," replied Tom, rather startled. " I'm sure *I'm* not much like Norman, any way."

" Do you mean to say that *I* am then ?" demanded Dick, blazing up. It was clear they had taken it into their heads that George, not Norman, was the hero of A. Z.'s story.

Seeing this, A. Z. laughed, and put a speedy stop to the rising heat.

" You're not a bit like Norman, either one of you," she said. " And as for being like George, in what was wrong in him I don't suppose you want to resemble him much ; in what was good and right you may both take him for an example if you like. And I don't see why either of you—or all three of you, boys, Frank included—may not be as good and as heroic as he was. He was neither very clever, nor very wise ; he was nothing but a brave true-hearted English lad (such as all of you might well be), who tried hard and lovingly to do his duty, and who did it straight on, thinking very little of himself by the way, till God took him home.

" And now children," said A. Z., rising up, " our last story is ended ; away with you and play."

She gathered her work together into her box as she spoke; but the children lingered for a moment or two about her chair.

" I'm sorry it's your last day, A. Z.," said blunt Tom.

And then it appeared that in their different ways they were all sorry, more or less, for they were good children enough, and A. Z. had done her best to be kind to them.

But their regrets did not take long to say, and in a minute their voices were all ringing loudly and merrily out on the lawn.

And A. Z. went up stairs and packed her trunks.

THE END.

Printed by R. & R. CLARK, *Edinburgh.*

ORIGINAL JUVENILE LIBRARY.

A CATALOGUE

OF

NEW AND POPULAR WORKS.

PRINCIPALLY FOR THE YOUNG.

Goldsmith Introduced to Newbery by Dr. Johnson.

PUBLISHED BY

GRIFFITH AND FARRAN,

(LATE GRANT AND GRIFFITH, SUCCESSORS TO NEWBERY AND HARRIS),

CORNER OF ST. PAUL'S CHURCHYARD,
LONDON.

WERTHEIMER AND CO., CIRCUS PLACE, FINSBURY CIRCUS.

STANESBY'S ILLUMINATED GIFT BOOKS.

Every page richly printed in Gold and Colours.

Aphorisms of the Wise and Good.

With a Photographic Portrait of Milton; intended as a companion volume to "Shakespeare's Household Words." Price 9s. cloth, elegant, 14s. Turkey morocco antique.

Shakespeare's Household Words;

With a Photographic Portrait taken from the Monument at Stratford-on-Avon. Price 9s. cloth elegant; 14s. morocco antique.

" An exquisite little gem, fit to be the Christmas offering to Titania or Queen Mab."— *The Critic.*

The Wisdom of Solomon;

From the Book of Proverbs. With a Photographic Frontispiece, representing the Queen of Sheba's visit to Solomon. Small 4to, price 14s. cloth elegant; 18s. calf; 21s. morocco antique.

The Bridal Souvenir;

Containing the Choicest Thoughts of the Best Authors, in Prose and Verse. New Edition, with a Portrait of the Princess Royal. Elegantly bound in white and gold, price 21s.

"A splendid specimen of decorative art, and well suited for a bridal gift."—*Literary Gazette.*

The Birth-Day Souvenir;

A Book of Thoughts on Life and Immortality, from Eminent Writers Small 4to. price 12s. 6d. illuminated cloth; 18s. morocco antique.

Light for the Path of Life;

From the Holy Scriptures. New and Improved Edition. Small 4to, price 12s. cloth elegant; 15s. calf gilt edges; 18s. morocco antique.

NEW BOOK OF EMBLEMS.

Square 8vo. price 21s. cloth elegant ; 27s., calf extra, 31s. 6d., morocco antique; beautifully printed by Whittingham, in Old English type, with the initial letters and borders in red.

𝔖piritual 𝔆onceits;

Extracted from the Writings of the Fathers, the old English Poets, etc , with One Hundred entirely New Designs, forming Symbolical Illustrations to the passages, by W. HARRY ROGERS.

" A book of deep thought and beautiful, yet quaint, artistic work."—*Art Journal.*

NEW AND POPULAR WORKS.

Memorable Battles in English History.
Where Fought, why Fought, and their Results. With Lives of the Commanders. By W. H. DAVENPORT ADAMS, author of "Neptune's Heroes; or, the Sea-kings of England." Frontispiece by ROBERT DUDLEY. Post 8vo. price 7s. 6d. extra cloth.

Our Soldiers;
Or, Anecdotes of the Campaigns and Gallant Deeds of the British Army during the reign of Her Majesty Queen Victoria. By W. H. G. KINGSTON. With Frontispiece from a Painting in the Victoria Cross Gallery. Fcp. 8vo. price 3s. cloth; 3s. 6d. gilt edges.

Our Sailors;
Or, Anecdotes of the Engagements and Gallant Deeds of the British Navy during the reign of Her Majesty Queen Victoria. By W. H. G. KINGSTON. With Frontispiece. Fcap. 8vo. price 3s. cloth; 3s. 6d. gilt edges.

A Hand-Book of the History of the United States.
Including the Colonial Period; War of Independence; Constitution of the States; Slavery and other Causes leading to the present War. By HUGO REID, late Principal of Dalhousie College, Halifax, Nova Scotia. Fcap. 8vo. price 2s. 6d. cloth.

My Grandmother's Budget
of Stories and Verses. By FRANCES FREELING BRODERIP, author of "Tiny Tadpole," etc. Illustrated by her brother, THOMAS HOOD. Price 3s. 6d. cloth; 4s. 6d. coloured, gilt edges.

The Loves of Tom Tucker and Little Bo-Peep.
Written and Illustrated by THOMAS HOOD. Quarto, price 2s. 6d. coloured plates.

Scenes and Stories of the Rhine.
By M. BETHAM EDWARDS, author of "Holidays among the Mountains," etc. With Illustrations by F. W. KEYL. Super Royal 16mo. price 3s. 6d. cloth; 4s. 6d. coloured, gilt edges.

Nursery Fun;
Or, the Little Folks' Picture Book. The Illustrations by C. H. BENNETT. Quarto, price 2s. 6d. coloured plates.

Play-Room Stories;
Or, How to make Peace. By GEORGIANA M. CRAIK. With Illustrations by C. GREEN. Super Royal 16mo. price 3s. 6d. cloth; 4s. 6d. coloured, gilt edges.

Fickle Flora,

and her Sea Side Friends. By EMMA DAVENPORT, author of "Live Toys," etc. With Illustrations by J. Absolon. Super Royal 16mo. price 3s. 6d. cloth; 4s. 6d. coloured, gilt edges.

The Faithful Hound.

A Story in Verse, founded on fact. By LADY THOMAS. With Illustrations by H. WEIR. Imperial 16mo, price 2s. 6d. cloth; 3s. 6d. coloured, gilt edges.

DEDICATED BY PERMISSION TO ALFRED TENNYSON.

The Story of King Arthur,

and his Knights of the Round Table. With Six Beautiful Illustrations, by G. H. THOMAS. Post 8vo. price 7s. cloth; 9s. coloured, gilt edges.

"Heartily glad are we to welcome the glorious old tale in its present shape."—*Gentleman's Magazine.*

NEW WORK BY ELWES.

Guy Rivers;

Or, a Boy's Struggles in the Great World. By ALFRED ELWES, Author of "Ralph Seabrooke," "Paul Blake." etc. With Illustrations by H. ANELAY. Fcap. 8vo. price 5s. cloth; 5s. 6d. gilt edges.

"Mr. Elwes sustains his reputation. The moral tone is excellent, and boys will derive from it both pleasure and profit."—*Athenæum.*

Ralph Seabrooke;

Or, The Adventures of a Young Artist in Piedmont and Tuscany. By ALFRED ELWES, Illustrated by DUDLEY. Fcap. 8vo.; price 5s. cloth; 5s. 6d. gilt edges.

Frank and Andrea;

Or Forest Life in the Island of Sardinia. By ALFRED ELWES. Illustrated by DUDLEY. Fcap. 8vo. Price 5s. cloth; 5s. 6d. gilt edges.

" The descriptions of Sardinian life and scenery are admirable."—*Athenæum.*

Paul Blake;

Or, the Story of a Boy's Perils in the Islands of Corsica and Monte Cristo. By ALFRED ELWES, Illustrated by H. ANELAY. Fcap. 8vo, price 5s. cloth; 5s. 6d. cloth, gilt edges.

"This spirited and engaging story will lead our young friends to a very intimate acquaintance with the island of Corsica."—*Art Journal.*

THOMAS HOOD'S DAUGHTER.

Tiny Tadpole;

And other Tales. By FRANCES FREELING BRODERIP, daughter of the late Thomas Hood. With Illustrations by HER BROTHER. Super-Royal 16mo. price 3s. 6d. cloth; 4s. 6d. coloured, gilt edges.

"A remarkable book, by the brother and sister of a family in which genius and fun are inherited."—*Saturday Review.*

Funny Fables for Little Folks.

By FRANCES FREELING BRODERIP. Illustrated by her Brother. Super Royal 16mo. price 2s. 6d. cloth; 3s. 6d. coloured, gilt edges.

" The Fables contain the happiest mingling of fun, fancy, humour, and instruction."— *Art Journal.*

CAPTAIN MARRYAT'S DAUGHTER.

Harry at School;

By EMILIA MARRYAT. With Illustrations by ABSOLON. Super Royal 16mo. price 2s. 6d. cloth; 3s. 6d. coloured, gilt edges.

"Really good, and fitted to delight little boys."—*Spectator.*

Long Evenings;

Or, Stories for My Little Friends, by EMILIA MARRYAT. Illustrated by ABSOLON, price 2s. 6d. cloth; 3s. 6d. coloured, gilt edges.

BY THE AUTHOR OF " TRIUMPHS OF STEAM."

Meadow Lea;

Or, the Gipsy Children; a Story founded on fact. By the Author of " The Triumphs of Steam," "Our Eastern Empire." etc. With Illustrations by JOHN GILBERT. Fcap. 8vo. price 4s. 6d. cloth; 5s. gilt edges.

Live Toys;

Or, Anecdotes of our Four-legged and other Pets. By EMMA DAVENPORT. With Illustrations by HARRISON WEIR. Super Royal 16mo. price 2s. 6d. cloth; 3s. 6d. coloured, gilt edges.

" One of the best kind of books for youthful reading."—*Guardian.*

Distant Homes;

Or, the Graham Family in New Zealand. By Mrs. J. E. AYLMER. With Illustrations by J. JACKSON. Super Royal 16mo. price 3s. 6d. cloth; 4s. 6d. coloured, gilt edges.

"English children will be delighted with the history of the Graham Family, and be enabled to form pleasant and truthful conceptions of the 'Distant Homes' inhabited by their kindred."—*Athenæum.*

Neptune's Heroes: or The Sea Kings of England;

from Hawkins to Franklin. By W. H. DAVENPORT ADAMS. Illustrated by MORGAN. Fcap. 8vo; price 5s. cloth; 5s. 6d. gilt edges.

"We trust Old England may ever have writers as ready and able to interpret to her children the noble lives of her greatest men."—*Athenaum.*

Lost in Ceylon;

The Story of a Boy and Girl's Adventures in the Woods and Wilds of the Lion King of Kandy. By WILLIAM DALTON. Illustrated by WEIR. Fcap. 8vo. price 5s. cloth; 5s. 6d. gilt edges.

The White Elephant;

Or the Hunters of Ava, and the King of the Golden Foot. By W. DALTON. Illustrated by WEIR. Fcap. 8vo. price 5s. cloth; 5s. 6d. gilt edges.

"Full of dash, nerve and spirit, and withal freshness."—*Literary Gazette.*

The War Tiger;

Or, The Adventures and Wonderful Fortunes of the Young Sea-Chief and his Lad Chow. By WILLIAM DALTON, Illustrated by H. S. MELVILLE. Fcap. 8vo, price 5s. cloth; 5s. 6d. cloth, gilt edges.

"A tale of lively adventure, vigorously told, and embodying much curious information." *Illustrated News.*

Holidays Among the Mountains;

Or, Scenes and Stories of Wales. By M. BETHAM EDWARDS. Illustrated by F. J. SKILL. Super royal 16mo.; price 3s. 6d. cloth; 4s. 6d. coloured, gilt edges.

E. LANDELLS.

The Illustrated Paper Model Maker;

Containing Twelve Pictorial Subjects, with Descriptive Letter-press and Diagrams for the construction of the Models. By E. LANDELLS. Price 2s. in a neat Envelope.

" A most excellent mode of educating both eye and hand in the knowledge of form."— *English Churchman.*

The Girl's Own Toy Maker,

And Book of Recreation. By E. LANDELLS, Author of "Home Pastime," etc., assisted by his daughter, ALICE LANDELLS. Second edition. With 200 Illustrations. Royal 16mo. price 2s. 6d. cloth.

" A perfect magazine of information."—*Illustrated News of the World.*

The Boy's own Toy Maker.

A Practical Illustrated Guide to the useful employment of Leisure Hours. By E. LANDELLS. With Two Hundred Cuts. Fourth Edition. Royal 16mo, price 2s. 6d., cloth.

" A new and valuable form of endless amusement."—*Nonconformist.*
" We recommend it to all who have children to be instructed and amused."—*Economist.*

Home Pastime;

Or, The Child's Own Toy Maker. With practical instructions. By E. LANDELLS. New and Cheaper Edition, price 3s. 6d. complete, with the Cards, and Descriptive Letterpress.

*** By this novel and ingenious "Pastime," Twelve beautiful Models can be made by Children from the Cards, by attending to the Plain and Simple Instructions in the Book.

" As a delightful exercise of Ingenuity, and a most sensible mode of passing a winter's evening, we commend the Child's own Toy Maker."—*Illustrated News.*
" Should be in every house blessed with the presence of children."—*The Field.*

The Triumphs of Steam;

Or, Stories from the Lives of Watt, Arkwright, and Stephenson. With Illustrations by J. GILBERT. Dedicated by permission to Robert Stephenson, Esq., M.P. Second edition. Royal 16mo, price 3s. 6d. cloth; 4s. 6d., coloured, gilt edges.

" A most delicious volume of examples."—*Art Journal.*

Our Eastern Empire;

Or, Stories from the History of British India. Second Edition, with Continuation to the Proclamation of Queen Victoria. With Four Illustrations. Royal 16mo. cloth 3s. 6d.; 4s. 6d. coloured, gilt edges.

" These stories are charming, and convey a general view of the progress of our Empire in the East. The tales are told with admirable clearness."—*Athenæum*.

The Martyr Land;

Or, Tales of the Vaudois. Frontispiece by J. GILBERT. Royal 16mo; price 3s. 6d. cloth.

" While practical lessons run throughout, they are never obtruded; the whole tone is refined without affectation, religious and cheerful."—*English Churchman*.

Might not Right;

Or, Stories of the Discovery and Conquest of America. Illustrated by J. Gilbert. Royal 16mo. price 3s. 6d. cloth; 4s. 6d. coloured, gilt edges.

" With the fortunes of Columbus, Cortes, and Pizarro, for the staple of these stories, the writer has succeeded in producing a very interesting volume."—*Illustrated News*.

Tuppy;

Or the Autobiography of a Donkey. By the Author of " The Triumphs of Steam," etc., etc. Illustrated by HARRISON WEIR. Super Royal 16mo. price 2s. 6d. cloth; 3s. 6d. coloured, gilt edges.

" A very intelligent donkey, worthy of the distinction conferred upon him by the artist." —*Art Journal*.

Hand Shadows,

To be thrown upon the Wall. A Series of Eighteen Original Designs. By HENRY BURSILL. 4to price 2s plain; 2s. 6d. coloured.

A Second Series of Hand Shadows;

With Eighteen New Subjects. By H. BURSILL. Price 2s. plain; 2s. 6d. coloured.

" Uncommonly clever—some wonderful effects are produced."—*The Press*.

THE LATE THOMAS HOOD, ETC.

Fairy Land;

Or, Recreation for the Rising Generation, in Prose and Verse. By THOMAS and JANE HOOD Illustrated by T. Hood, Jun. Super royal 16mo; price 3s. 6d. cloth; 4s. 6d. coloured gilt edges.

The Headlong Career and Woful Ending of Preco-

CIOUS PIGGY. Written for his Children, by the late THOMAS HOOD. With a Preface by his Daughter; and Illustrated by his Son. Third Edition. Post 4to, fancy boards, price 2s. 6d., coloured.

" The Illustrations are intensely humourous."—*The Critic.*

The History of a Quartern Loaf.

in Rhymes and Pictures. By WILLIAM NEWMAN. 12 Illustrations. Price 6d. plain, 1s. coloured. 2s. 6d. on linen, and bound in cloth.

Uniform in size and price,

The History of a Cup of Tea.

The History of a Scuttle of Coals.

The History of a Lump of Sugar.

A Woman's Secret;

Or How to Make Home Happy. 23rd Thousand. 18mo. price 6d.

By the same Author, uniform in size and price,

Woman's Work; or, How she can Help the Sick.

13th Thousand.

A Chapter of Accidents;

Or, the Mother's Assistant in cases of Burns, Scalds, Cuts, &c.

Pay To-day, Trust To-morrow;

A Story illustrative of the Evils of the Tally System. 4th Thousand.

Nursery Work;

Or Hannah Baker's First Place. 4th Thousand.

Family Prayers for Cottage Homes;

With a Few Words on Prayer, and Select Scripture Passages. Fcap. 8vo. price 4d. limp cloth.

*** These little works are admirably adapted for circulation among the working classes.

The Fairy Tales of Science.

A Book for Youth. By J. C. BROUGH. With 16 Beautiful Illustrations by C. H. BENNETT. Fcap. 8vo, price 5s., cloth; 5s. 6d. gilt edges.

CONTENTS: 1. The Age of Monsters.—2. The Amber Spirit.—3. The Four Elements.—4. The Life of an Atom.—5. A Little Bit.—6. Modern Alchemy.—7. The Magic of the Sunbeam.—8. Two Eyes Better than One.—9. The Mermaid's Home.—10. Animated Flowers.—11. Metamorphoses.—12. The Invisible World.—13. Wonderful Plants. 14. Water Bewitched.—15. Pluto's Kingdom.—16. Moving Lands.—17. The Gnomes.—18. A Flight through Space.—19. The Tale of a Comet.—20. The Wonderful Lamp.

" Science, perhaps, was never made more attractive and easy of entrance into the youthful mind."—*The Builder.*
" Altogether the volume is one of the most original, as well as one of the most useful, books of the season."—*Gentleman's Magazine.*

The Nine Lives of a Cat;

A Tale of Wonder. Written and Illustrated by C. H. BENNETT. Twenty-four Engravings. Imperial 16mo. price 2s. cloth; 2s. 6d. coloured.

" Rich in the quaint humour and fancy that a man of genius knows how to spare for the enlivenment of children."—*Examiner.*

Sunday Evenings with Sophia;

Or, Little Talks on Great Subjects. A Book for Girls. By LEONORA G. BELL. Frontispiece by J. ABSOLON. Fcap. 8vo, price 2s. 6d. cloth.

" A very suitable gift for a thoughtful girl."—*Bell's Messenger.*

Blind Man's Holiday;

Or Short Tales for the Nursery. By the Author of " Mia and Charlie," "Sidney Grey," etc. Illustrated by John Absolon. Super Royal 16mo. price 3s. 6d. cloth; 4s. 6d. coloured, gilt edges.
" Very true to nature and admirable in feeling."—*Guardian.*

Scenes of Animal Life and Character.

From Nature and Recollection. In Twenty Plates. By J. B. 4to, price 2s., plain; 2s. 6d., coloured, fancy boards.

" Truer, heartier, more playful, or more enjoyable sketches of animal life could scarcely be found anywhere."—*Spectator.*

Caw, Caw;

Or, the Chronicles of the Crows. Illustrated by J. B. 4to, price 2s. plain; 2s. 6d. coloured.

Jack Frost and Betty Snow;

With other Tales for Wintry Nights and Rainy Days. Illustrated by H. Weir. 2s. 6d. cloth; 3s. 6d. coloured, gilt edges.

" The dedication of these pretty tales, prove by whom they are written; they are indelibly stamped with that natural and graceful method of amusing while instructing, which only persons of genius possess."—*Art Journal.*

W. H. G. KINGSTON'S BOOKS FOR BOYS

With Illustrations. Fcap. 8vo. price 5s. each, cloth; 5s. 6d. gilt edges.

True Blue;

Or, the Life and Adventures of a British Seaman of the Old School.

"There is about all Mr. Kingston's tales a spirit of hopefulness, honesty, and cheery good principle, which makes them most wholesome, as well as most interesting reading."—*Era.*

Will Weatherhelm;

Or, the Yarn of an Old Sailor about his Early Life and Adventures.

"We tried the story on an audience of boys, who one and all declared it to be capital."—*Athenæum.*

Fred Markham in Russia;

Or, the Boy Travellers in the Land of the Czar.

"Most admirably does this book unite a capital narrative, with the communication of valuable information respecting Russia."—*Nonconformist.*

Salt Water;

Or Neil D'Arcy's Sea Life and Adventures. With Eight Illustrations.

"With the exception of Capt. Marryat, we know of no English author who will compare with Mr. Kingston as a writer of books of nautical adventure."—*Illustrated News.*

Manco, the Peruvian Chief;

With Illustrations by CARL SCHMOLZE.

"A capital book; the story being one of much interest, and presenting a good account of the history and institutions, the customs and manners, of the country."—*Literary Gazette.*

Mark Seaworth;

A Tale of the Indian Ocean. By the Author of "Peter the Whaler," etc. With Illustrations by J. ABSOLON. Second Edition.

"No more interesting, nor more safe book, can be put into the hands of youth; and to boys especially, 'Mark Seaworth' will be a treasure of delight."—*Art Journal.*

Peter the Whaler;

His early Life and Adventures in the Arctic Regions. Second Edition. Illustrations by E. DUNCAN.

"A better present for a boy of an active turn of mind could not be found. The tone of the book is manly, healthful, and vigorous."—*Weekly News.*

"A book which the old may, but which the young must, read when they have once begun it."—*Athenæum.*

Old Nurse's Book of Rhymes, Jingles, and Ditties.

Illustrated by C. H. BENNETT. With Ninety Engravings. Fcap. 4to. price 3s. 6d. cloth, plain, or 6s. coloured.

"The illustrations are all so replete with fun and imagination, that we scarcely know who will be most pleased with the book, the good-natured grandfather who gives it, or the chubby grandchild who gets it, for a Christmas-Box."—*Notes and Queries*.

Maud Summers the Sightless:

A Narrative for the Young. Illustrated by Absolon. 3s. 6d. cloth; 4s. 6d. coloured, gilt edges.

"A touching and beautiful story."—*Christian Treasury*.

Clara Hope;

Or, the Blade and the Ear. By Miss MILNER. With Frontispiece by Birket Foster. Fcap. 8vo. price 3s. 6d. cloth; 4s. 6d. cloth elegant, gilt edges.

"A beautiful narrative, showing how bad habits may be eradicated, and evil tempers subdued."—*British Mother's Journal*.

The Adventures and Experiences of Biddy Dork-

ING and of the FAT FROG. Edited by Mrs. S. C. HALL. Illustrated by H. Weir. 2s. 6d. cloth; 3s. 6d. coloured, gilt edges.

"Most amusingly and wittily told."—*Morning Herald*.

BY THE AUTHOR OF "CAT AND DOG," ETC.

Historical Acting Charades;

Or, Amusements for Winter Evenings. New Edition. Fcap. 8vo. price 3s. 6d. cloth; 4s. gilt edges.

"A rare book for Christmas parties, and of practical value."—*Illustrated News*.

The Story of Jack and the Giants:

With thirty-five Illustrations by RICHARD DOYLE. Beautifully printed. New and Cheaper Edition. Fcap. 4to. price 2s. 6d. cloth; 3s. 6d. coloured, extra cloth, gilt edges.

"In Doyle's drawings we have wonderful conceptions, which will secure the book a place amongst the treasures of collectors, as well as excite the imaginations of children."—*Illustrated Times*.

Granny's Wonderful Chair;

And its Tales of Fairy Times. By FRANCES BROWNE. With Illustrations by KENNY MEADOWS. Small 4to, 3s. 6d. cloth, 4s. 6d. coloured, gilt edges.

"One of the happiest blendings of marvel and moral we have ever seen."—*Literary Gazette.*

The Early Dawn;

Or, Stories to Think about. By a COUNTRY CLERGYMAN. Illustrated by H. WEIR, etc. Small 4to.; price 2s. 6d. cloth; 3s. 6d. coloured, gilt edges.

"The matter is both wholesome and instructive, and must fascinate as well as benefit the young."—*Literarium.*

Angelo;

Or, the Pine Forest among the Alps. By GERALDINE E. JEWSBURY, author of "The Adopted Child," etc. With Illustrations by JOHN ABSOLON. Small 4to; price 2s. 6d. cloth; 3s. 6d. coloured, gilt edges.

"As pretty a child's story as one might look for on a winter's day."—*Examiner.*

Tales of Magic and Meaning.

Written and Illustrated by ALFRED CROWQUILL, Author of "Funny Leaves for the Younger Branches," "The Careless Chicken," "Picture Fables," etc. Small 4to.; price 3s. 6d. cloth; 4s. 6d. coloured.

"Cleverly written, abounding in frolic and pathos, and inculcates so pure a moral, that we must pronounce him a very fortunate little fellow, who catches these 'Tales of Magic,' as a windfall from 'The Christmas Tree'."—*Athenæum.*

Faggots for the Fire Side;

Or, Tales of Fact and Fancy. By PETER PARLEY. With Twelve Tinted Illustrations. Foolscap 8vo.; 3s. 6d., cloth; 4s. gilt edges.

"A new book by Peter Parley is a pleasant greeting for all boys and girls, wherever the English language is spoken and read. He has a happy method of conveying information, while seeming to address himself to the imagination."—*The Critic.*

The Discontented Children;

And How they were Cured. By MARY and ELIZABETH KIRBY. Illustrated by H. K. BROWNE (Phiz.). Second edition, price 2s. 6d. cloth; 3s. 6d. coloured, gilt edges.

"We know no better method of banishing 'discontent' from school-room and nursery than by introducing this wise and clever story to their inmates."—*Art Journal.*

The Talking Bird;

Or, the Little Girl who knew what was going to happen. By M. and E. KIRBY. With Illustrations by H. K. BROWNE (PHIZ). Small 4to. Price 2s. 6d. cloth; 3s. 6d. coloured, gilt edges.

" The story is ingeniously told, and the moral clearly shown."—*Athenæum.*

Julia Maitland;

Or, Pride goes before a Fall. By M. and E. KIRBY. Illustrated by ABSOLON. Price 2s. 6d. cloth; 3s. 6d. coloured, gilt edges.

"It is nearly such a story as Miss Edgeworth might have written on the same theme."— *The Press.*

Letters from Sarawak,

Addressed to a Child; embracing an Account of the Manners, Customs, and Religion of the Inhabitants of Borneo, with Incidents of Missionary Life among the Natives. By Mrs. M'DOUGALL. Fourth Thousand, with Illustrations. 3s. 6d. cloth.

A" is new, interesting, and admirably told."—*Church and State Gazette.*

COMICAL PICTURE BOOKS.

Uniform in size with "The Struwwelpeter."

Each with Sixteen large Coloured Plates, price 2s. 6d., in fancy boards, or mounted on cloth, 1s. extra.

Picture Fables.

Written and Illustrated by ALFRED CROWQUILL.

The Careless Chicken;

By the BARON KRAKEMSIDES. By ALFRED CROWQUILL.

Funny Leaves for the Younger Branches.

By the BARON KRAKEMSIDES, of Burstenoudelafen Castle. Illustrated by ALFRED CROWQUILL.

Laugh and Grow Wise;

By the Senior Owl of Ivy Hall. With Sixteen large coloured Plates. Price 2s. 6d. fancy boards; or 3s. 6d. mounted on cloth.

The Remarkable History of the House that Jack

Built. Splendidly Illustrated and magnificently Illuminated by THE SON OF A GENIUS. Price 2s. in fancy cover.

"Magnificent in suggestion, and most comical in expression!"—*Athenæum.*

A Peep at the Pixies;

Or, Legends of the West. By Mrs. BRAY. Author of "Life of Stothard," "Trelawny," etc., etc. With Illustrations by Phiz. Super-royal 16mo, price 3s. 6d. cloth; 4s. 6d. coloured, gilt edges.

"A peep at the actual Pixies of Devonshire, faithfully described by Mrs. Bray, is a treat. Her knowledge of the locality, her affection for her subject, her exquisite feeling for nature, and her real delight in fairy lore, have given a freshness to the little volume we did not expect. The notes at the end contain matter of interest for all who feel a desire to know the origin of such tales and legends."—*Art Journal.*

A BOOK FOR EVERY CHILD.

The Favourite Picture Book;

A Gallery of Delights, designed for the Amusement and Instruction of the Young. With several Hundred Illustrations from Drawings by J. ABSOLON, H. K. BROWNE (Phiz), J. GILBERT, T. LANDSEER, J. LEECH, J. S. PROUT, H. WEIR, etc. New Edition. Royal 4to., price 3s. 6d., bound in a new and Elegant Cover; 7s. 6d. coloured; 10s. 6d. mounted on cloth and coloured.

Ocean and her Rulers;

A Narrative of the Nations who have from the earliest ages held dominion over the Sea; and comprising a brief History of Navigation. By ALFRED ELWES. With Frontispiece. Fcap. 8vo, 5s. cloth; 5s. 6d. gilt edges.

"The volume is replete with valuable and interesting information; and we cordially recommend it as a useful auxiliary in the school-room, and entertaining companion in the library."—*Morning Post.*

Berries and Blossoms.

A Verse Book for Children. By T. WESTWOOD. With Title and Frontispiece printed in Colours. Super-royal 16mo, price 3s. 6d. cloth, gilt edges.

The Wonders of Home, in Eleven Stories.

By GRANDFATHER GREY. With Illustrations. Third and Cheaper Edition. Royal 16mo., 2s. 6d. cloth; 3s. 6d. coloured, gilt edges.

CONTENTS.—1. The Story of a Cup of Tea.—2. A Lump of Coal.—3. Some Hot Water.—4. A Piece of Sugar.—5. The Milk Jug.—6. A Pin.—7. Jenny's Sash.—8. Harry's Jacket.—9. A Tumbler.—10. A Knife.—11. This Book.

" The idea is excellent, and its execution equally commendable. The subjects are well selected, and are very happily told in a light yet sensible manner."—*Weekly News*.

Cat and Dog;

Or, Memoirs of Puss and the Captain. Illustrated by WEIR. Sixth Edition. Super-royal 16mo, 2s. 6d. cloth; 3s. 6d. coloured, gilt edges.

" The author of this amusing little tale is, evidently, a keen observer of nature. The illustrations are well executed ; and the moral, which points the tale, is conveyed in the most attractive form."—*Britannia*.

The Doll and Her Friends;

Or, Memoirs of the Lady Seraphina. By the Author of " Cat and Dog." Third Edition. With Four Illustrations by H. K. BROWNE (Phiz). 2s. 6d., cloth; 3s. 6d. coloured, gilt edges.

"Evidently written by one who has brought great powers to bear upon a small matter."—*Morning Herald*.

Tales from Catland;

Dedicated to the Young Kittens of England. By an OLD TABBY. Illustrated by H. WEIR. Third Edition. Small 4to, 2s. 6d. plain; 3s. 6d. coloured, gilt edges.

" The combination of quiet humour and sound sense has made this one of the pleasantest little books of the season."—*Lady's Newspaper*.

The Grateful Sparrow.

A True Story, with Frontispiece. Third Edition. Price 6d. sewed.

How I Became a Governess.

By the Author of "The Grateful Sparrow." Second Edition. With Frontispiece. Price 1s. sewed.

Dicky Birds.

A True Story. By the same Author. With Frontispiece. Price 6d.

WORKS BY MRS. R. LEE.

Anecdotes of the Habits and Instincts of Animals.
Third and Cheaper Edition. With Illustrations by HARRISON WEIR. Fcap. 8vo, 3s. 6d. cloth; 4s. gilt edges.

Anecdotes of the Habits and Instincts of Birds,
REPTILES, and FISHES. With Illustrations by HARRISON WEIR. Second and Cheaper Edition. Fcap. 8vo, 3s. 6d. cloth; 4s. gilt edges.

"Amusing, instructive, and ably written."—*Literary Gazette.*
"Mrs. Lee's authorities—to name only one, Professor Owen—are, for the most part first-rate.'—*Athenæum.*

Twelve Stories of the Sayings and Doings of
ANIMALS. With Illustrations by J. W. ARCHER. Third Edition. Super-royal 16mo, 2s. 6d. cloth; 3s. 6d. coloured, gilt edges.

"It is just such books as this that educate the imagination of children, and enlist their sympathies for the brute creation."—*Nonconformist.*

Familiar Natural History.
With Forty-two Illustrations from Original Drawings by HARRISON WEIR. Super-royal 16mo, 3s. 6d. cloth; 5s. coloured gilt edges.

Playing at Settlers;
Or, the Faggot House. Illustrated by GILBERT. Second Edition. Price 2s. 6d. cloth; 3s. 6d. coloured, gilt edges.

Adventures in Australia;
Or, the Wanderings of Captain Spencer in the Bush and the Wilds. Second Edition. Illustrated by PROUT. Fcap. 8vo., 5s. cloth; 5s. 6d. gilt edges.

"This volume should find a place in every school library; and it will, we are sure, be a very welcome and useful prize."—*Educational Times.*

The African Wanderers;
Or, the Adventures of Carlos and Antonio; embracing interesting Descriptions of the Manners and Customs of the Western Tribes, and the Natural Productions of the Country. Third Edition. With Eight Engravings. Fcap. 8vo, 5s. cloth; 5s. 6d. gilt edges.

"For fascinating adventure, and rapid succession of incident, the volume is equal to any relation of travel we ever read."—*Britannia.*

"In strongly recommending this admirable work to the attention of young readers, we feel that we are rendering a real service to the cause of African civilization."—*Patriot.*

Sir Thomas; or, the Adventures of a Cornish
BARONET IN WESTERN AFRICA. With Illustrations by J. GILBERT. Fcap. 8vo.; 3s. 6d. cloth.

Harry Hawkins's H-Book;

Shewing how he learned to aspirate his H's. Frontispiece by H. WEIR. Second Edition. Super-royal 16mo, price 6d.

" No family or school-room within, or indeed beyond, the sound of Bow bells, should be without this merry manual."—*Art Journal.*

The Family Bible Newly Opened;

With Uncle Goodwin's account of it. By JEFFERYS TAYLOR, author of "A Glance at the Globe," etc. Frontispiece by J. GILBERT. Fcap. 8vo, 3s. 6d. cloth.

" A very good account of the Sacred Writings, adapted to the tastes, feelings, and intelligence of young people."—*Educational Times.*

Kate and Rosalind;

Or, Early Experiences. By the author of "Quicksands on Foreign Shores," etc. Fcap. 8vo, 3s. 6d. cloth; 4s. gilt edges.

" A book of unusual merit. The story is exceedingly well told, and the characters are drawn with a freedom and boldness seldom met with."—*Church of England Quarterly.*

" We have not room to exemplify the skill with which Puseyism is tracked and detected. The Irish scenes are of an excellence that has not been surpassed since the best days of Miss Edgeworth."—*Fraser's Magazine.*

Good in Everything;

Or, The Early History of Gilbert Harland. By MRS. BARWELL, Author of "Little Lessons for Little Learners," etc. Second Edition. With Illustrations by JOHN GILBERT. Royal 16mo., 2s. 6d. cloth; 3s. 6d., coloured, gilt edges.

" The moral of this exquisite little tale will do more good than a thousand set tasks abounding with dry and uninteresting truisms."—*Bell's Messenger.*

A Word to the Wise;

Or, Hints on the Current Improprieties of Expression in Writing and Speaking. By PARRY GWYNNE. 10th Thousand. 18mo. price 6d. sewed, or 1s. cloth. gilt edges.

" All who wish to mind their *p*'s and *q*'s should consult this little volume."—*Gentleman's Magazine.*

" May be advantageously consulted by even the well-educated."—*Athenæum.*

ELEGANT GIFT FOR A LADY.
Trees, Plants, and Flowers;

Their Beauties, Uses and Influences. By Mrs. R. LEE, Author of "The African Wanderers," etc. With beautiful coloured Illustrations by J. ANDREWS. 8vo, price 10s. 6d., cloth elegant, gilt edges.

"The volume is at once useful as a botanical work, and exquisite as the ornament of a boudoir table."—*Britannia.* "As full of interest as of beauty."—*Art Journal.*

NEW AND BEAUTIFUL LIBRARY EDITION.
The Vicar of Wakefield;

A Tale. By OLIVER GOLDSMITH. Printed by Whittingham. With Eight Illustrations by J. ABSOLON. Square fcap. 8vo, price 5s., cloth; 7s. half-bound morocco, Roxburghe style; 10s. 6d. antique morocco.

Mr. Absolon's graphic sketches add greatly to the interest of the volume: altogether, it is as pretty an edition of the 'Vicar' as we have seen. Mrs. Primrose herself would consider it 'well dressed.'"—*Art Journal.*

"A delightful edition of one of the most delightful of works: the fine old type and thick paper make this volume attractive to any lover of books."—*Edinburgh Guardian.*

WORKS BY MRS. LOUDON.
Domestic Pets;

Their Habits and Management; with Illustrative Anecdotes. By Mrs. LOUDON. With Engravings from Drawings by HARRISON WEIR. Second Thousand. Fcap. 8vo, 2s. 6d. cloth.

CONTENTS:—The Dog, Cat, Squirrel, Rabbit, Guinea-Pig. White Mice, the Parrot and other Talking Birds, Singing Birds, Doves and Pigeons, Gold and Silver Fish.

"A most attractive and instructive little work. All who study Mrs. Loudon's pages will be able to treat their pets with certainty and wisdom."—*Standard of Freedom.*

Glimpses of Nature;

And Objects of Interest described during a Visit to the Isle of Wight. Designed to assist and encourage Young Persons in forming habits of observation. By Mrs. LOUDON. Second Edition, enlarged. With Forty-one Illustrations. 3s. 6d. cloth.

"We could not recommend a more valuable little volume. It is full of information, conveyed in the most agreeable manner."—*Literary Gazette.*

Tales of School Life.

By AGNES LOUDON, Author of "Tales for Young People." With Illustrations by JOHN ABSOLON. Second Edition. Royal 16mo, 2s. 6d. plain; 3s. 6d. coloured, gilt edges.

"These reminiscences of school days will be recognised as truthful pictures of every-day occurrence. The style is colloquial and pleasant, and therefore well suited to those for whose perusal it is intended."—*Athenæum.*

MISS JEWSBURY.

Clarissa Donnelly;

Or, The History of an Adopted Child. By MISS GERALDINE E. JEWSBURY. With an Illustration by JOHN ABSOLON. Fcap. 8vo, 3s. 6d. cloth; 4s. gilt edges.

' With wonderful power, only to be matched by as admirable a simplicity, Miss Jewsbury has narrated the history of a child. For nobility of purpose, for simple, nervous writing, and for artistic construction, it is one of the most valuable works of the day."—*Lady's Companion.*

The Day of a Baby Boy;

A Story for a Young Child. By E. BERGER. With Illustrations by JOHN ABSOLON. Second Edition. Super-royal 16mo, price 2s. 6d. cloth; 3s. 6d. coloured, gilt edges.

" A sweet little book for the nursery."—*Christian Times.*

Every-Day Things;

Or, Useful Knowledge respecting the principal Animal, Vegetable, and Mineral Substances in common use. Written for Young Persons. Second Edition, revised. 18mo., 1s. 6d. cloth.

" A little encyc'opædia of useful knowledge, deserving a place in every juvenile library.' —*Evangelical Magazine.*

PRICE SIXPENCE EACH, PLAIN; ONE SHILLING, COLOURED.

In Super-Royal 16mo., beautifully printed, each with Seven Illustrations by HARRISON WEIR, *and Descriptions by* MRS. LEE.

1. BRITISH ANIMALS. First Series.
2. BRITISH ANIMALS. Second Series.
3. BRITISH BIRDS.
4. FOREIGN ANIMALS. First Series.
5. FOREIGN ANIMALS. Second Series.
6. FOREIGN BIRDS.

*** Or bound in One Volume under the title of "Familiar Natural History," *see page* 17.

Uniform in size and price with the above.

THE FARM AND ITS SCENES. With Six Pictures from Drawings by HARRISON WEIR.

THE DIVERTING HISTORY OF JOHN GILPIN. With Six Illustrations by WATTS PHILLIPS.

THE PEACOCK AT HOME, AND BUTTERFLY'S BALL. With Four Illustrations by HARRISON WEIR.

WORKS BY THE AUTHOR OF MAMMA'S BIBLE STORIES.

Fanny and her Mamma;

Or, Easy Lessons for Children. In which it is attempted to bring Scriptural Principles into daily practice. Illustrated by J. GILBERT. Third Edition. 16mo, 2s. 6d. cloth; 3s. 6d. coloured, gilt edges.

"A little book in beautiful large clear type, to suit the capacity of infant readers, which we can with pleasure recommend."—*Christian Ladies' Magazine.*

Short and Simple Prayers,

For the Use of Young Children. With Hymns. Fifth Edition. Square 16mo, 1s. 6d. cloth.

"Well adapted to the capacities of children—beginning with the simplest forms which the youngest child may lisp at its mother's knee, and proceeding with those suited to its gradually advancing age. Special prayers, designed for particular circumstances and occasions, are added. We cordially recommend the book."—*Christian Guardian.*

Mamma's Bible Stories,

For her Little Boys and Girls, adapted to the capacities of very young Children. Eleventh Edition, with Twelve Engravings. 2s. 6d. cloth; 3s. 6d. coloured, gilt edges.

A Sequel to Mamma's Bible Stories.

Fifth Edition. Twelve Illustrations. 2s. 6d. cloth, 3s. 6d. coloured.

Scripture Histories for Little Children.

With Sixteen Illustrations, by JOHN GILBERT. Super-royal 16mo, price 3s. cloth; 4s. 6d. coloured, gilt edges.

CONTENTS.—The History of Joseph—History of Moses—History of our Saviour—The Miracles of Christ.

Sold separately: 6d. each, plain; 1s. coloured.

Bible Scenes;

Or, Sunday Employment for very young Children. Consisting of Twelve Coloured Illustrations on Cards, and the History written in Simple Language. In a neat box, 3s. 6d.; or the Illustrations dissected as a Puzzle, 6s. 6d.

FIRST SERIES: JOSEPH.   SECOND SERIES: OUR SAVIOUR.
THIRD SERIES: MOSES.   FOURTH SERIES: MIRACLES OF CHRIST.

"It is hoped that these 'Scenes' may form a useful and interesting addition to the Sabbath occupations of the Nursery. From their very earliest infancy little children will listen with interest and delight to stories brought thus palpably before their eyes by means of illustration."—*Preface.*

ILLUSTRATED BY GEORGE CRUIKSHANK.

Kit Bam, the British Sinbad;

Or, the Yarns of an Old Mariner. By MARY COWDEN CLARKE, author of "The Concordance to Shakspeare," etc. Fcap. 8vo, price 3s. 6d. cloth; 4s. gilt edges.

"A more captivating volume for juvenile recreative reading we never remember to have seen. It is as wonderful as the 'Arabian Nights,' while it is free from the objectionable matter which characterises the Eastern fiction."—*Standard of Freedom.*
"Cruikshank's plates are worthy of his genius."—*Examiner.*

The Favourite Library.

A Series of Works for the Young; each Volume with an Illustration by a well-known Artist. Price 1s. cloth.

1. THE ESKDALE HERD BOY. By LADY STODDART.
2. MRS. LEICESTER'S SCHOOL. By CHARLES and MARY LAMB.
3. THE HISTORY OF THE ROBINS. By MRS. TRIMMER.
4. MEMOIR OF BOB, THE SPOTTED TERRIER.
5. KEEPER'S TRAVELS IN SEARCH OF HIS MASTER.
6. THE SCOTTISH ORPHANS. By LADY STODDART.
7. NEVER WRONG; or, THE YOUNG DISPUTANT; and "IT WAS ONLY IN FUN."
8. THE LIFE AND PERAMBULATIONS OF A MOUSE.
9. EASY INTRODUCTION TO THE KNOWLEDGE OF NATURE. By MRS. TRIMMER.
10. RIGHT AND WRONG. By the Author of "ALWAYS HAPPY."
11. HARRY'S HOLIDAY. By JEFFERYS TAYLOR.
12. SHORT POEMS AND HYMNS FOR CHILDREN.

The above may be had Two Volumes bound in One, at Two Shillings cloth, or 2s. 6d. gilt edges, as follows:—

1. LADY STODDART'S SCOTTISH TALES.
2. ANIMAL HISTORIES. THE DOG.
3. ANIMAL HISTORIES. THE ROBINS and MOUSE.
4. TALES FOR BOYS. HARRY'S HOLIDAY and NEVER WRONG.
5. TALES FOR GIRLS. MRS. LEICESTER'S SCHOOL and RIGHT AND WRONG.
6. POETRY AND NATURE. SHORT POEMS and TRIMMER'S INTRODUCTION.

Stories of Julian and his Playfellows.

Written by HIS MAMMA. With Four Illustrations by JOHN ABSOLON. Second Edition. Small 4to., 2s. 6d., plain; 3s. 6d., coloured, gilt edges.

"The lessons taught by Julian's mamma are each fraught with an excellent moral."—*Morning Advertiser.*

Blades and Flowers.

Poems for Children. Frontispiece by ANELAY. Fcap. 8vo; price 2s. cloth.

"Breathing the same spirit as the Nursery Poems of Jane Taylor."—*Literary Gazette.*

Aunt Jane's Verses for Children.

By Mrs. T. D. CREWDSON. Illustrated with twelve beautiful Engravings. Fcap. 8vo; 3s. 6d. cloth.

"A charming little volume, of excellent moral and religious tendency."—*Evangelical Magazine.*

Rhymes of Royalty.

The History of England in Verse, from the Norman Conquest to the reign of QUEEN VICTORIA; with an Appendix, comprising a summary of the leading events in each reign. Fcap. 8vo, with Frontispiece. 2s. 6d. cloth.

NEW AND CHEAPER EDITION.

The Ladies' Album of Fancy Work.

Consisting of Novel, Elegant, and Useful Patterns in Knitting, Netting, Crochet, and Embroidery, printed in Colours. Bound in a beautiful cover. New Edition. Post 4to, 3s. 6d., gilt edges.

Visits to Beechwood Farm;

Or, Country Pleasures. By CATHERINE M. A. COUPER. Illustrations by ABSOLON. Small 4to, 3s. 6d., plain; 4s. 6d. coloured; gilt edges.

"The work is well calculated to impress upon the minds of the young the superiority of simple and natural pleasures over those which are artificial."—*Englishwoman's Magazine.*

The Modern British Plutarch;

Or, Lives of Men distinguished in the recent History of our Country for their Talents, Virtues and Achievements. By W. C. TAYLOR, LL.D. Author of "A Manual of Ancient and Modern History," etc. 12mo, Second Thousand, with a new Frontispiece. 4s. 6d. cloth; 5s. gilt edges.

CONTENTS: Arkwright — Burke — Burns — Byron · Canning — Earl of Chatham — Adam Clarke — Clive — Captain Cook — Cowper — Crabbe — Davy — Eldon — Erskine — Fox · · Franklin — Goldsmith — Earl Grey — Warren Hastings — Heber — Howard — Jenner — Sir W. Jones — Mackintosh — H. Martyn — Sir J. Moore — Nelson — Pitt — Romilly — Sir. W. Scott — Sheridan — Smeaton — Watt — Marquis of Wellesley — Wilberforce — Wilkie — Wellington.

"A work which will be welcomed in any circle of intelligent young persons."—*British Quarterly Review.*

Home Amusements.

A Choice Collection of Riddles, Charades, Conundrums, Parlour Games, and Forfeits. By PETER PUZZLEWELL, Esq., of Rebus Hall. New Edition, revised and enlarged, with Frontispiece by H. K. BROWNE (Phiz). 16mo, 2s. 6d. cloth.

Early Days of English Princes.

By Mrs. RUSSELL GRAY. Dedicated by permission to the Duchess of Roxburgh. With Illustrations by JOHN FRANKLIN. Small 4to., 3s. 6d. cloth; 4s. 6d. coloured, gilt edges.

"Just the book for giving children some first notions of English history, as the personages it speaks about are themselves young."—*Manchester Examiner*.

First Steps in Scottish History,

By MISS RODWELL, Author of "First Steps to English History." With Ten Illustrations by WEIGALL. 16mo, 3s. 6d. cloth; 4s. 6d. coloured.

"It is the first popular book in which we have seen the outlines of the early history of the Scottish tribes exhibited with anything like accuracy."—*Glasgow Constitutional*.

"The work is throughout agreeably and lucidly written."—*Midland Counties Herald*.

London Cries and Public Edifices.

Illustrated in Twenty-four Engravings by LUKE LIMNER; with descriptive Letter-press. Square 12mo, 2s. 6d. plain; 5s. coloured. Bound in emblematic cover.

The Silver Swan;

A Fairy Tale. By MADAME DE CHATELAIN. Illustrated by JOHN LEECH. Small 4to, 2s. 6d. cloth; 3s. 6d. coloured, gilt edges.

"The moral is in the good, broad, unmistakeable style of the best fairy period."—*Athenæum*.

"The story is written with excellent taste and sly humour."—*Atlas*.

Mrs. Trimmer's Concise History of England,

Revised and brought down to the present time by Mrs. MILNER. With Portraits of the Sovereigns in their proper costume, and Frontispiece by HARVEY. New Edition in One Volume. 5s. cloth.

"The editing has been very judiciously done. The work has an established reputation for the clearness of its genealogical and chronological tables, and for its pervading tone of Christian piety."—*Church and State Gazette*.

The Celestial Empire;

or, Points and Pickings of Information about China and the Chinese. By the late "OLD HUMPHREY." With Twenty Engravings from Drawings by W. H. PRIOR. Fcap. 8vo, 3s. 6d., cloth; 4s. gilt edges.

" This very handsome volume contains an almost incredible amount of information."— *Church and State Gazette.*

" The book is exactly what the author proposed it should be, full of good information, good feeling, and good temper."—*Allen's Indian Mail.*

"Even well-known topics are treated with a graceful air of novelty,"—*Athenæum.*

Tales from the Court of Oberon.

Containing the favourite Histories of Tom Thumb, Graciosa and Percinet, Valentine and Orson, and Children in the Wood. With Sixteen Illustrations by ALFRED CROWQUILL. Small 4to, 2s. 6d. plain; 3s. 6d. coloured.

True Stories from Ancient History,

Chronologically arranged from the Creation of the World to the Death of Charlemagne. Twelfth Edition. With 24 Steel Engravings. 12mo, 5s. cloth.

True Stories from Modern History,

Chronologically arranged from the Death of Charlemagne to the present Time. Eighth Edition. With 24 Steel Engravings. 12mo, 5s. cloth.

True Stories from English History,

Chronologically arranged from the Invasion of the Romans to the Present Time. Sixth Edition. With 36 Steel Engravings. 12mo, 5s. cloth.

Stories from the Old and New Testaments,

On an improved plan. By the Rev. B. H. DRAPER. With 48 Engravings. Fifth Edition. 12mo, 5s. cloth.

Wars of the Jews,

As related by JOSEPHUS; adapted to the Capacities of Young Persons, With 24 Engravings. Sixth Edition. 4s. 6d. cloth.

The Prince of Wales' Primer.

With 300 Illustrations by J. GILBERT. Dedicated to her Majesty. New Edition, price 6d.; with title and cover printed in gold and colours, 1s.

Pictorial Geography.

For the use of Children. Presenting at one view Illustrations of the various Geographical Terms, and thus imparting clear and definite ideas of their meaning. On a Large Sheet. Price 2s. 6d. in tints; 5s. on Rollers, varnished.

One Thousand Arithmetical Tests;

Or, The Examiner's Assistant. Specially adapted, by a novel arrangement of the subject, for Examination Purposes, but also suited for general use in Schools. By T. S. CAYZER, Head Master of Queen Elizabeth's Hospital, Bristol. Price 1s. 6d. cloth.

*** Answers to the above, 1s, 6d. cloth.

THE ABBÉ GAULTIER'S GEOGRAPHICAL WORKS.

I. Familiar Geography.

With a concise Treatise on the Artificial Sphere, and two coloured Maps, illustrative of the principal Geographical Terms. Fifteenth Edition. 16mo, 3s. cloth.

II. An Atlas.

Adapted to the Abbé Gaultier's Geographical Games, consisting of 8 Maps coloured, and 7 in Outline, etc. Folio, 15s. half-bound.

Butler's Outline Maps, and Key;

Or, Geographical and Biographical Exercises; with a Set of Coloured Outline Maps; designed for the Use of Young Persons. By the late WILLIAM BUTLER. Enlarged by the author's son, J. O. BUTLER. Thirty-second Edition, revised. 4s.

Rowbotham's New and Easy Method of Learning

the FRENCH GENDERS. New Edition. 6d.

Bellenger's French Word and Phrase-book.

Containing a select Vocabulary and Dialogues, for the Use of Beginners. New Edition, 1s. sewed.

MARIN DE LA VOYE'S ELEMENTARY FRENCH WORKS.

Les Jeunes Narrateurs;

Ou Petits Contes Moraux. With a Key to the difficult words and phrases. Frontispiece. Second Edition. 18mo, 2s. cloth.
"Written in pure and easy French."—*Morning Post.*

The Pictorial French Grammar;

For the Use of Children. With Eighty Illustrations. Royal 16mo., price 1s. sewed; 1s. 6d. cloth.

Le Babillard.

An Amusing Introduction to the French Language. By a French Lady. Sixth Edition. 2s. cloth.

Der Schwätzer;

Or, the Prattler. An amusing Introduction to the German Language, on the Plan of "Le Babillard." 16 Illustrations. 16mo, price 2s. cloth.

Battle Fields.

A graphic Guide to the Places described in the History of England as the scenes of such Events; with the situation of the principal Naval Engagements fought on the Coast of the British Empire. By Mr. WAUTHIER, Geographer. On a large sheet 3s. 6d.; in case 6s., or on a roller, and varnished, 9s.

Tabular Views of the Geography and Sacred History of PALESTINE, and of the TRAVELS of ST. PAUL.

Intended for Pupil Teachers, and others engaged in Class Teaching. By A. T. WHITE. Oblong 8vo, price 1s., sewed.

The First Book of Geography;

Specially adapted as a Text Book for Beginners, and as a Guide to the Young Teacher. By HUGO REID, author of "Elements of Astronomy," etc. Third Edition, carefully revised. 18mo, 1s. sewed.
"One of the most sensible little books on the subject of Geography we have met with."
—*Educational Times.*

The Child's Grammar,

By the late LADY FENN, under the assumed name of Mrs. Lovechild. Forty-ninth Edition. 18mo, 9d. cloth.

Always Happy;

Or, Anecdotes of Felix and his Sister Serena. By the author of "Claudine," etc. Eighteenth Edition, with new Illustrations. Royal 18mo, price 2s. 6d. cloth.

Andersen's (H. C.) Nightingale and other Tales.

2s. 6d. plain; 3s. 6d. coloured.

Anecdotes of Kings,

Selected from History; or, Gertrude's Stories for Children. With Engravings. 2s. 6d. plain; 3s. 6d. coloured.

Bible Illustrations;

Or, a Description of Manners and Customs peculiar to the East, and especially Explanatory of the Holy Scriptures. By the Rev. B. H. DRAPER. With Engravings. Fourth Edition. Revised by J. KITTO, Editor of "The Pictorial Bible," etc. 3s. 6d. cloth.

"This volume will be found unusually rich in the species of information so much needed by young readers of the Scriptures."—*Christian Mother's Magazine.*

The British History briefly told,

and a Description of the Ancient Customs, Sports, and Pastimes of the English. Embellished with full-length Portraits of the Sovereigns of England in their proper Costumes, and 18 other Engravings. 3s. 6d. cloth.

Chit-chat;

Or, Short Tales in Short Words. By a MOTHER, author of "Always Happy." New Edition. With Eight Engravings. Price 2s. 6d. cloth, 3s. 6d. coloured, gilt edges.

Conversations on the Life of Jesus Christ.

For the use of Children. By a MOTHER. A new Edition. With 12 Engravings. 2s. 6d. plain; 3s. 6d. coloured.

Cosmorama.

The Manners, Customs, and Costumes of all Nations of the World described. By J. ASPIN. New Edition with numerous Illustrations. 3s. 6d. plain; and 4s. 6d. coloured.

Easy Lessons;

Or, Leading-Strings to Knowledge. New Edition, with 8 Engravings. 2s. 6d. plain; 3s. 6d. coloured, gilt edges.

Key to Knowledge;

Or, Things in Common Use simply and shortly explained. By a MOTHER, Author of "Always Happy," etc. Thirteenth Edition. With Sixty Illustrations. 3s. 6d. cloth.

Facts to correct Fancies;

Or, Short Narratives compiled from the Biography of Remarkable Women. By a MOTHER. With Engravings, 3s. 6d. plain; 4s. 6d. coloured.

Fruits of Enterprise;

Exhibited in the Travels of Belzoni in Egypt and Nubia. Thirteenth Edition, with six Engravings. 18mo, price 3s. cloth.

The Garden;

Or, Frederick's Monthly Instructions for the Management and Formation of a Flower Garden. Fourth Edition. With Engravings of the Flowers in Bloom for each Month in the Year, etc. 3s. 6d. plain; or 6s. with the Flowers coloured.

How to be Happy;

Or, Fairy Gifts: to which is added a Selection of Moral Allegories, from the best English Writers. With Steel Engravings. Price 3s. 6d. cloth.

Infantine Knowledge.

A Spelling and Reading Book, on a Popular Plan, combining much Useful Information with the Rudiments of Learning. By the Author of "The Child's Grammar." With numerous Engravings. Ninth Edition. 2s. 6d. plain; 3s. 6d. coloured, gilt edges.

The Ladder to Learning.

A Collection of Fables, Original and Select, arranged progressively in words of One, Two, and Three Syllables. Edited and improved by the late Mrs. TRIMMER. With 79 Cuts. Nineteenth Edition. 3s. 6d. cloth.

Little Lessons for Little Learners.

In Words of One Syllable. By Mrs. BARWELL. Ninth Edition, with numerous Illustrations. 2s. 6d. plain; 3s. 6d. coloured, gilt edges.

The Little Reader.

A Progressive Step to Knowledge. Fourth Edition with sixteen Plates. Price 2s. 6d. cloth.

Mamma's Lessons.

For her Little Boys and Girls. Thirteenth Edition, with eight Engravings. Price 2s. 6d. cloth; 3s. 6d. coloured, gilt edges.

The Mine;

Or, Subterranean Wonders. An Account of the Operations of the Miner and the Products of his Labours; with a Description of the most important in all parts of the World. By the late Rev. ISAAC TAYLOR. Sixth Edition, with numerous corrections and additions by Mrs. LOUDON. With 45 new Woodcuts and 16 Steel Engravings. 3s. 6d. cloth.

Young Jewess, The, and her Christian School-

fellows. By the Author of "Rhoda," etc. With a Frontispiece by J. GILBERT. 16mo, 1s. cloth.

Rhoda;

Or, The Excellence of Charity. Fourth Edition. With Illustrations. 16mo, 2s. cloth.

The Rival Crusoes,

And other Tales. By AGNES STRICKLAND, author of "The Queens of England." Sixth Edition. 18mo, price 2s. 6d. cloth.

Short Tales.

Written for Children. By DAME TRUELOVE and her Friends. A new Edition, with 20 Engravings. 3s. 6d. cloth.

The Students;

Or, Biographies of the Grecian Philosophers. 12mo, price 2s. 6d. cloth.

Stories of Edward and his little Friends.

With 12 Illustrations. Second Edition. 3s. 6d. plain; 4s. 6d. coloured.

Sunday Lessons for little Children.

By Mrs. BARWELL. Third Edition. 2s. 6d. plain; 3s. coloured.

A Visit to Grove Cottage,

And the India Cabinet Opened. By the author of "Fruits of Enterprise." New Edition. 18mo, price 3s. cloth.

Dissections for Young Children;

In a neat box. Price 5s. each.

1. SCENES FROM THE LIVES OF JOSEPH AND MOSES.
2. SCENES FROM THE HISTORY OF OUR SAVIOUR.
3. OLD MOTHER HUBBARD AND HER DOG.
4. LIFE AND DEATH OF COCK ROBIN.

TWO SHILLINGS EACH, CLOTH.

ANECDOTES OF PETER THE GREAT, Emperor of Russia. 18mo.

COUNSELS AT HOME; with Anecdotes, Tales, &c.

MORAL TALES. By a FATHER. With 2 Engravings.

ONE SHILLING AND SIXPENCE EACH, CLOTH.

THE DAUGHTER OF A GENIUS. A Tale. By MRS. HOFLAND. Sixth Edition.

ELLEN THE TEACHER. By MRS. HOFLAND. New Edition.

THE SON OF A GENIUS. By MRS. HOFLAND. New Edition.

THEODORE; or, the Crusaders. By MRS. HOFLAND. New Edition.

SHORT AND SIMPLE PRAYERS FOR CHILDREN, WITH HYMNS. By the Author of "Mamma's Bible Stories," &c.

TRIMMER'S (MRS.) OLD TESTAMENT LESSONS. With 40 Engravings.

TRIMMER'S (MRS.) NEW TESTAMENT LESSONS. With 40 Engravings. New Editions.

ONE SHILLING, PLAIN. ONE SHILLING AND SIXPENCE, COLOURED.

THE DAISY, with Thirty Wood Engravings. 26th Edition.

THE COWSLIP, with Thirty Engravings. 24th Edition.

ONE SHILLING EACH. CLOTH.

WELCOME VISITOR; a Collection of Original Stories, &c.

NINA, an Icelandic Tale. By the Author of "Always Happy."

SPRING FLOWERS and the MONTHLY MONITOR.

THE HISTORY OF PRINCE LEE BOO. New Edition.

THE CHILD'S DUTY. Dedicated by a Mother to her Children. Second Edition.

DECEPTION and FREDERICK MARSDEN, the Faithful Friend.

LESSONS of WISDOM for the YOUNG. By the REV. W. FLETCHER.

DURABLE NURSERY BOOKS,

MOUNTED ON CLOTH WITH COLOURED PLATES,

ONE SHILLING EACH.

1 Alphabet of Goody Two-Shoes.
2 Cinderella.
3 Cock Robin.
4 Courtship of Jenny Wren.
5 Dame Trot and her Cat.
6 History of an Apple Pie.
7 House that Jack built.
8 Little Rhymes for Little Folks.

9 Mother Hubbard.
10 Monkey's Frolic.
11 Old Woman and her Pig.
12 Puss in Boots.
13 Tommy Trip's Museum of Birds, Part I.
14 ——————————— Part II.

DURABLE BOOKS FOR SUNDAY READING.

SCENES FROM THE LIVES OF JOSEPH AND MOSES. Illustrated by J. GILBERT. Printed on linen. Price 6d..
SCENES FROM THE LIFE OF OUR SAVIOUR. Illustrated by J. GILBERT. Printed on linen. Price 6d.

DARNELL'S EDUCATIONAL WORKS.

The attention of all interested in the subject of Education is invited to these Works, now in extensive use throughout the Kingdom, prepared by Mr. Darnell, a Schoolmaster of many years' experience.

1. COPY BOOKS.—A SHORT AND CERTAIN ROAD TO A GOOD HAND-WRITING, gradually advancing from the Simple Stroke to a superior Small-hand.

LARGE POST, Sixteen Numbers, 6d. each.

FOOLSCAP, Twenty Numbers, to which are added Three Supplementary Numbers of Angular Writing for Ladies, and One of Ornamental Hands. Price 3d. each.

  ⁎ This series may also be had on very superior paper, marble covers, 4d. each.

" For teaching writing I would recommend the use of Darnell's Copy Books. I have noticed a marked improvement wherever they have been used."—*Report of Mr. Maye* (*National Society's Organizer of Schools*) *to the Worcester Diocesan Board of Education.*

2. GRAMMAR, made intelligible to Children, price 1s. cloth.

3. ARITHMETIC, made intelligible to Children, price 1s. 6d. cloth.
  ⁎ Key to Parts 2 and 3, price 1s. cloth.

4. READING, a Short and Certain Road to, price 6d. cloth.

GRIFFITH AND FARRAN, CORNER OF ST. PAUL'S CHURCHYARD.

WERTHEIMER AND CO , CIRCUS PLACE, FINSBURY CIRCUS.